ADVENTU

THE MYSTERY
OF THE
PHANTOM LIGHTS

Carrickstowe

N

Grand Vista
Hotel

Tregower
Hamlet

Sunset
Lodge

Westward
Beach

Quarr

Chapel

Pendragon
Manor

SOUTH

MOOR

Shepherd's
Hut

West Rock
Beach

Keyhole Cove

Pencarrick
Point

CASTLE

KEY

MAINLAND

THE CAUSEWAY

Wheel Power Test Track

Hollow Tree

North Point

NORTH MOOR

Tin Mine

Standing Stones

Roshendra Farm & Stables

Willow Island

Chicken Bay

Polhallow Lake

Black Rock Island

Common

Bosgoose Wood

Forgotten Cove

Stone Cottage

Inn

Park

Castle

Village Green

Hall

Dotty's

Coastguard Cottage

Ice Works

Whistling Caves

Trago Gallery

KEY BAY

Pirate Cove

Shipwreck The Mermaid

Abandoned Monastery

The Lighthouse

Shipwreck

Collect all the Adventure Island *books*

ADVENTURE ISLAND

THE MYSTERY OF THE PHANTOM LIGHTS

Helen Moss

Illustrated by Leo Hartas

Orion
Children's Books

First published in Great Britain in 2013
by Orion Children's Books
a division of the Orion Publishing Group Ltd
Orion House
5 Upper St Martin's Lane
London WC2H 9EA
An Hachette UK company

1 3 5 7 9 10 8 6 4 2

Text copyright © Helen Moss 2013
Map and interior illustrations copyright
© Leo Hartas 2013

The Orion Publishing Group's policy is to use papers
that are natural, renewable and recyclable products and
made from wood grown in sustainable forests. The logging
and manufacturing processes are expected to conform to
the environmental regulations of the country of origin.

A catalogue record for this book
is available from the British Library.

ISBN 978 1 4440 0758 9

Printed in Great Britain by Clays Ltd, St Ives plc

For Rosie Armitage,
winner of Operation Diamond

One

Night Fright!

Camping out on the moors was awesome, Jack Carter thought.

Until, that was, you woke up at two o'clock in the morning with an urgent need to go to the bathroom.

The moors were distinctly lacking in the bathroom department.

Which is why Jack was now stumbling around in the

dark searching for a conveniently placed gorse bush. A boy needed his privacy!

Mission accomplished, Jack stepped out from behind the bush and started back towards the tents, which were pitched on a flat patch of grass and heather halfway down a rocky slope. He picked his way over the rough ground. Although it had been a scorching August day, the night air was chilly. He shivered and sped up; his sleeping bag was calling to him.

That's when he slipped on a loose stone and fell flat on his face.

And that's when he realized he couldn't see the tents.

He must have strayed farther from camp than he'd thought. In fact, he wasn't sure he was even heading in the right direction! He sat up, trying to get his bearings.

It was so dark that he could hardly make out the outline of the craggy ridge that rose up from the other side of the valley; it was just a smudge of blacker blackness against the black sky. And it was very quiet. *Too quiet!* Jack was a Londoner, used to streetlights and a soundtrack of car engines, sirens and snatches of music. Although he and his older brother, Scott, had been coming to stay with their great-aunt Kate for the holidays on the remote island of Castle Key for ages, while their dad was off on his archaeological digs, he still couldn't get used to all this nocturnal peace and quiet.

Jack looked back the way he'd come. Now he could make out the outline of the tents in the distance, lit by the faint amber glow of nightlights through the canvas. He stood up and hurried towards them.

Now he was on the right track again, he started hatching a plan.

Obviously, he was going to have to creep around outside the tent he was sharing with Scott and make some spooky noises. It would be a crime to miss this golden opportunity to give his brother a fright! Should he go for a ghostly wail, he wondered, or a snarling werewolf effect? The key thing was to make sure he got the right tent. (He'd learned that lesson the hard way on the school camping trip to Hatfield Forest, when he'd accidentally performed his entire mutant zombie scarecrow routine for his elderly geography teacher, Miss Bodley, instead of his mates, Josh and Ali. The shriek she'd produced when he lurched into her tent and shuffled round her sleeping bag had nearly burst his eardrums! There'd been letters home, detentions and grounding.)

But there was no danger of getting muddled this time; Jack and Scott's tent was a little apart from the rest of the group, next to the one that housed their friend, Emily Wild, and her faithful dog, Drift. And Emily's tent was hard to miss! It was more of a shelter than a tent, consisting only of sticks, leaves and a canvas sheet. And there was a rainwater catcher and a handcrafted washstand outside it. Emily liked to practise her survival skills whenever possible, in case she was suddenly called up by the security forces and sent off on a top-secret undercover mission in the wilderness. Scott and Jack had tried pointing out that, as she was only thirteen years old, this was unlikely to happen any time soon. But, as was so often the case, Emily didn't listen.

The remaining three tents belonged to other members of the Castle Key Nature Group. They'd all been taking part in a glow-worm survey. Nature had never really been Jack's thing, but earlier in the summer he and Scott and Emily had gone to see a pair of killer whales off North Point and, before they knew it, they'd been railroaded into joining the group. It had actually turned out to be very useful in solving the mysterious disappearance of an amazing supercar called the Black Salamander. Don Penrose, the group leader, had even awarded them gold Nature Watch badges! It turned out that glow-worms weren't real worms; they were beetles with luminous bums. It *had* been cool, though, when they'd finally spotted the tiny lights gleaming in the undergrowth.

Jack wasn't far from the tents and had just made up his mind to treat Scott to a bone-chilling werewolf howl when he heard a noise behind him.

A strange snuffling, shuffling noise.

He stopped in his tracks.

Maybe it was Scott or Emily trying to scare him. Or Drift out for a walk. But it couldn't be. Jack had kept his eyes fixed on the tents all the way back. He'd have noticed if anyone had come out.

There it was again! The noise was closer now. It sounded like the grinding of enormous teeth.

Jack's heart began to pound as if trying to break out of his ribcage with a sledgehammer.

Was it a *beast*? All these wild moor-type places had *beasts* prowling around ... A Bigfoot or a Yeti or a giant black panther with massive fangs like a sabre-toothed tiger ready to tear him limb from limb. He wanted to make a run for the tents but his legs seemed to think they were trapped in quicksand and were refusing to work. Jack closed his eyes and wished he were somewhere else – somewhere safe, somewhere with lights and shops and houses – somewhere like London ...

The beast was so close Jack could smell its meaty breath.

It was no good. He had to see what was about to eat him. Slowly, *very* slowly, he turned round.

His trembling torch beam picked out a pair of long, curved horns. Jack gulped. It wasn't just a beast, it was a *demon* beast! But then he saw the soft white ears, the big brown eyes, the long black and white face with the slightly dopey expression ...

Jack laughed out loud. He'd noticed the herd of goats earlier in the evening. They belonged to Roshendra Farm, and were let loose on the high moors to graze.

'Give me some warning next time you creep up on me, mate!' Jack said. 'I was that close to having to overpower you with my grip of death!'

The goat blinked and worked its jaws from side to side.

Jack patted the goat's neck and was turning to leave when he noticed three bright lights in the sky. White and red and green, they zoomed so low that they barely skimmed the ridge across the valley. They circled round and round, then hovered in one spot, shimmering and flashing, lighting up the shreds of cloud that floated in front of them with shades of blood red and ghostly green.

Below them, another light flickered on and off and darted about.

Jack stared at the lights. What were they? They were too bright and colourful for planets or stars, and you'd have to have a death wish to fly a plane that low over the ridge. But they were hovering too long to be fireworks. Could it be a helicopter? Surely he'd have heard the whirr of the rotors. And then there was the single light dancing beneath the others, almost as if it were calling to them.

Suddenly Jack knew what he was looking at: a UFO! An *Unidentified Flying Object* visiting Earth from a far-off planet! It was the only logical explanation. Just wait until Scott and Emily heard about this!

The lights seemed to be coming closer.

Uh-oh, Jack thought. He'd seen a programme on TV about alien abductions. Aliens beamed people up into their spaceships and experimented on them.

Jack didn't want to be an experiment.

'I don't know about you,' he whispered to the goat, 'but I'm out of here!'

But when he turned round, the goat had vanished!

Two

Looking for Evidence

'What are you talking about?' Scott groaned, pulling his sleeping bag over his head.

Jack shook his brother by the shoulders and told him again.

Scott sat up and yawned. He peered at his watch. It was two fifteen. 'You saw some lights?' he repeated. 'And a load of aliens have kidnapped a goat. What would they want a *goat* for?'

'Experiments, of course!' Jack said. 'You should know. You're always playing that game on your phone …'

Scott rolled his eyes. 'That's aliens abducting *cows*, not goats. And anyway it's just a game.'

'Yeah, well, perhaps they've got enough cows now and they've moved on to other farm animals. All I know is that one second the goat was right behind me – I was talking to it – and the next second there were these spooky lights and the goat had vanished into thin air!'

'*You were talking to the goat?*' Scott snorted. 'This just keeps getting better.' He laughed. 'If the aliens were looking for intelligent life on Earth and it was a choice between you and a goat, I guess they made a good call.'

'Ha ha!' Jack snapped, furious with himself for letting the talking-to-goats part slip out. What was he thinking? It must be the shock! He gave Scott another shake. 'Come and have a look.'

Scott burrowed back into his sleeping bag.

'Suit yourself,' Jack grumbled. 'I'm sure *Emily* will be interested in an alien abduction.'

—

'Lights on the moors?' Emily echoed, leaping out of her sleeping bag. She was fully dressed in a black tracksuit. In a single move, she grabbed a head torch, a camera and a pair of night-vision goggles from the investigation kit she always kept in her shoulder bag, and called to Drift, who'd been curled up next to her, dreaming about

16

squirrels. 'It's probably smugglers,' she whispered, as she jogged away from the camp. 'They must be signalling that it's safe for their boat to come into land.'

'Why would they be signalling two miles from the coast?' Jack panted, as he ran to catch up with her.

Emily stopped and turned to Jack, dazzling him with her head torch. Her long dark curls were more tangled than ever, springing out at all angles. She sighed. 'Yeah, good point.'

Jack, Emily and Drift stared out into the night, listening to the muffled roar and sputter of a motorbike on a distant road. The strange lights in the sky had gone.

Jack pointed in the direction of the ridge. 'I swear they were right there!'

'Did you get a photo?' Emily asked.

Jack shook his head.

Emily sighed. 'Compass bearings?'

'Believe it or not, I don't usually take a camera and compass when I go to the loo in the middle of the night.'

'Why not? It's important to be prepared to record evidence at all times.'

Jack was about to laugh when he realized Emily was deadly serious.

⁓

Next morning, after packing up camp, the friends hiked to Roshendra Farm where they'd left their bikes. Drift hopped up into his special basket on the back of Emily's bike and they cycled back to Castle Key village.

They headed straight for Dotty's Tea Rooms on the seafront, settled down at a table outside and ordered cooked breakfasts all round. Camping was hungry work!

Although it was still early, the morning was already warm. The sun sparkled on the waves that lapped against the fishing boats in the harbour, and gulls soared and swooped in a sky of clearest blue.

While they waited for their food, Jack recounted the story of the strange lights yet again. He remembered to leave out his conversation with the goat this time.

'You sure you weren't just dreaming about giant glow-worms?' Scott laughed.

Jack flicked a sugar cube at his brother. Annoyingly, Scott ducked at the last minute and it flew past his ear and hit the man at the next table. To Jack's relief, it bounced off the sleeve of his leather motorbike jacket and he didn't notice.

'Is it a bird?' Scott intoned in a dramatic Superman-movie voice. 'Is it a plane? No, it's the invasion of the goat-snatchers from outer space!'

Jack ignored him. 'I'm going to report it on one of those UFO sighting websites,' he said. In fact, he'd gone over the events of the night so many times in his head that he was now almost sure he'd witnessed at least ten lights spinning in formation and a horde of eerie green alien beings, scouring the moors for Earth-based life-forms to beam up to their flying saucer for their grisly experiments. He should probably call the local news stations. This time tomorrow he could be on the Breakfast TV sofa reliving his narrow escape from the extraterrestrial tentacles ...

'It could have been a spy plane,' Emily suggested, her dark eyes gleaming with excitement. She loved spies almost as much as smugglers.

'Spying on *what*, exactly?' Scott laughed. 'There's nothing up on the moors except sheep and goats.' He slapped his forehead as if he'd just had a brilliant idea. 'Of course! It was a rival goat farmer trying to steal the secrets of Roshendra Farm's award-winning goat's cheese!'

Emily giggled. She didn't believe Jack's story about aliens either, but she was sure Jack had seen *something* on the moors. If he'd made the whole thing up as a joke, he definitely wouldn't have been able to resist telling them by now!

So what *were* those lights? Could they have been something to do with the stories her friend Old Bob the fisherman used to tell her? Unlike Scott and Jack, Emily had grown up in Castle Key, in the old lighthouse which her parents ran as a Bed and Breakfast. 'There are legends about people seeing spooky *phantom lights* on the moors,' she said. 'Some say they're the lanterns of the piskey folk or that they're restless spirits rising up from Stone Age burial sites. Not that I believe any of that stuff, of course,' she added quickly.

'No way!' Jack spluttered. 'I was *not* seeing pixies!

Or fairies or gnomes with little pointy hats! Do you think I'm *nuts* or something?'

Scott was about to answer that when Dotty appeared with three plates of sausage, bacon, eggs and beans. The café owner wore her usual red and white polka-dot apron over her jeans and t-shirt, and her blonde hair was tied in a long plait. She gave them all a friendly smile as she placed the plates on the table.

'If you've seen the phantom lights on the moors you'd best stay well away,' she warned. 'The spirits play tricks. They lead people away from the paths into dangerous bogs and ravines.'

'Right!' Scott said with a grin as he reached for the salt. 'We'll bear that in mind.'

But Dotty wasn't laughing. In fact, she looked seriously worried as she handed Jack a full bottle of tomato sauce before hurrying back to the counter.

Scott shrugged. He was used to hearing spooky island legends from old-timers like Old Bob, but he hadn't expected a normal, young twenty-first century person – who listened to Beyoncé and Jessie J on her iPod and drove a cool red Mini – to be so superstitious.

'I've had a brainwave,' Jack said through a mouthful of bacon. 'Let's go up to the moors and look for evidence of the aliens.'

Scott rolled his eyes. 'You think we'll find a big ring of scorched earth where their spaceship landed?'

But Emily was in! Jack had said the magic words *look*

for evidence. Looking for evidence was one of Emily's all-time favourite activities. Ever since they'd wrapped up the baffling case of the Keepers of the Key, she'd been on the lookout for a new investigation. This could be it! She pushed her plate away, passed her last sausage under the table to Drift, and took her notebook – a smart black one with a thin red stripe – out of her bag. She turned to the first page, wrote *OPERATION PHANTOM LIGHTS* neatly at the top and underlined it twice in red – using her ruler, of course.

Scott almost choked on his baked beans. 'I can't wait to see the suspect list! One – aliens; two – pixies; three – restless spirits.'

'Nobody's forcing you to join this investigation. Emily and I make a perfectly good crime-busting duo without you.' Jack looked at Drift, who was hoping for another sausage. 'Sorry, Drifty, I meant a *trio*!'

Scott grinned. This wasn't a *real* investigation, but on the trillion-to-one chance that there *had* actually been an alien invasion last night, he didn't want to be left out. 'Alright,' he said. 'I suppose I'd better come along and make sure you don't get into trouble.'

Even Emily – who had been exploring the island all her life – hadn't realized quite how vast the high moors to the north of the disused quarry were until she started

21

conducting a fingertip search for signs of alien activity.

Starting from last night's campsite, the friends ran down the hill and waded across the stream that tumbled and skipped over its bed of smooth stones at the bottom of the valley. They scrambled up the rugged slope on the other side, following Jack's directions – which were vague to say the least. Everywhere had looked different in the dark.

The higher they climbed, the more treacherous the ground became. Even the tufts of purple heather could barely cling on here. The friends fanned out and searched separately – every rock, gully, crag and crevasse along the ridge.

Every few minutes Jack would shout, 'I'm sure it was around here somewhere!' But it never was.

'We're never going to find anything!' Scott grumbled.

Drift raced between the three of them, enjoying the extra-long afternoon walk.

At last, Emily stopped at the top of a steep slope. She flopped down on a flat rock and took her bottle of water from her bag. It was almost empty. Hot and tired after slipping and sliding over the loose scree, she was starting to agree with Scott. There was nothing here!

Then she heard Jack shouting from behind an outcrop of rock.

Another false alarm! she thought.

'You'll never believe it!' Jack yelled. 'The aliens crash-landed!'

Three

Crash Landing

Scott and Emily found Jack standing at the edge of a ravine that sliced the ground like a knife wound. It wasn't exactly the Grand Canyon – but it was as long as a football pitch and far too wide to jump across. It was also very deep.

'See!' Jack crowed, hopping up and down. 'I *told* you there was a UFO!'

Lost for words, Scott and Emily could only stare. It

was clear that *something* had plummeted from the skies and met a terrible end in the jaws of the chasm.

Wreckage lay scattered on the floor of the ravine and several springs and coils of wire and misshapen steel struts had caught on snags of rock on the way down, where they now hung like ghoulish Christmas decorations. A large section of the craft had stuck halfway down, its ends wedged firmly against the sides of the rift.

Emily knelt and began snapping photographs. She reached down to touch one of the shards of metal suspended near the top of the ravine. Jack grabbed her arm and wrestled her away.

'Don't touch,' he cried. 'It's probably protected by some weird extraterrestrial technology that's lethal to humans.'

Without a word, Emily reached into her bag, pulled out a pair of latex gloves, a surgical mask and a pair of tweezers, and continued her scene-of-crime inspection.

Jack lay on his stomach and peered down into the chasm. *This explains everything!* he thought. *The aliens must have crashed just after beaming up the goat. No wonder they didn't come back for me.* Suddenly he glimpsed a movement in the wreckage. He froze, torn between running away and staying to look. Were alien death-beasts about to leap out and zap him with their cosmic blasters? But, what if just one alien had survived the impact, and was stranded all alone on a hostile planet?

I could befriend the poor little guy, Jack thought. *It would be just like in that film, E.T.* He pictured himself on the first day back at school, introducing his new buddy. 'Yeah, this is Zok. He's from Mars, actually.' It would be so cool!

But to Jack's great disappointment, when the 'alien' emerged, it was nothing more than a nosy magpie, scavenging among the wreckage, and his dreams of inter-planetary friendship were crushed.

Meanwhile, Scott was also taking a closer look. Something didn't add up. 'This crash didn't happen last night,' he said. 'The metal's all rusty.'

Jack shrugged. 'So? The spacecraft obviously wasn't designed to withstand the Earth's atmosphere. The metal is decaying much faster than normal.'

Scott laughed. 'Nice try! But since when did flying saucers have propellers?'

Emily peeled off her gloves and mask. Scott was right, of course. She'd been so swept up by Jack's UFO theory that she'd failed to notice that plant roots had twined around the coils of wire. Heather and grass had grown up through the gaps in the metal. The wreckage had been here for years.

'This was a small aeroplane,' Scott was saying. 'That long piece lodged halfway down looks like the wing. You can even see a bit of the red, white and blue RAF target pattern on it.'

'It must be the plane that crashed here during World

War Two,' Emily said. 'Old Bob told me he saw it happen when he was a kid. It was on its way back from a bombing raid in Germany. It was badly damaged and came down over the ridge.' She paused and shuddered. 'The three airmen were all killed. People say their ghosts roam the moors at night.'

Scott turned to Jack. 'Maybe *that's* what you saw last night,' he teased. 'The gho-o-o-o-st plane with its phantom crew.'

Jack made a harrumphing noise. He was still trying to get over the loss of his new friend, Zok.

But Emily had seen something interesting at the edge of the ravine. 'Look at this!' she said, bending so that her nose almost touched the ground. 'There are some footprints here.'

'Ooh, *alien* footprints?' Jack crouched next to her, hoping for something with fifteen toes or a grossly shaped sucker or two ...

'I don't think so!' Emily laughed. 'Not unless they were wearing human shoes. These prints were made by ordinary flat-soled boots or trainers with a criss-cross pattern on the sole.'

'Probably just someone out on a hike,' Scott said. 'Maybe they stopped here to have a look at the wreckage.'

But these footprints were the only 'evidence' Emily had to work with and she was going to make the most of them. She inspected them through her magnifying glass and photographed them with her phone camera. Then she took a tape measure from her bag and measured them. 'Two hundred and fifty-five millimetres long,' she murmured. 'That's a size six and a half.'

Jack and Scott exchanged glances. 'And you just happened to know that?' Jack asked.

Emily flipped to the back of her notebook. 'There's a simple conversion table,' she said, holding it up to show them. 'Just one of the basics that any good investigator should know!'

'Six and a half?' Scott said. 'That's a bit small for a man's shoe. It was probably a woman.'

'Look at Drift!' Jack cried all of a sudden. 'He's freaking out!' Emily looked. Jack was right. Drift was backing away from the ravine on his belly, shaking his head and growling. His ears were flat to his head and the fur on his hackles was standing on end.

Emily ran to Drift and gave him a hug. 'It's OK,' she murmured into his fur. 'Don't be scared. I'm here.' She looked up at the boys. 'Perhaps he's picking up the ghosts of those World War Two airmen! Animals can sense things.'

Drift licked her nose. He didn't know anything about ghosts. He was just relieved that Emily, Scott and Jack were finally moving away from that ravine. He could feel in his paws that the ground along the edge was unstable and could crumble away at any moment. Drift was amazed they couldn't sense it – but then humans were strange like that. They seemed to have no sense of smell or direction either. Just to make sure they didn't go near the ravine again he ran around, herding them like a sheepdog.

Jack and Scott laughed as Drift headbutted their knees to urge them along.

'I think he wants us to get out of here,' Jack said.

'I'm with you, Drift,' Scott added. 'There's nothing to see here. Let's face it, Jack was just imagining those lights last night.'

Emily stuffed her notebook back into her bag.

It seemed that Operation Phantom Lights had reached a dead end.

—

Scott and Emily may have given up on Operation Phantom Lights but Jack wasn't going to be beaten that easily. He was determined to get to the bottom of the mystery and he was perfectly capable of conducting an investigation alone.

The next morning at Stone Cottage he found an old notebook that Aunt Kate had used for shopping lists. Equipped with a blunt pencil and a box of Jaffa Cakes, he settled down on the sofa in the living room, switched on the television – which was showing *Top Gear*, one of his favourite programmes – balanced the notebook on his knees and set to work.

First he wrote *OPERATION FANTOM LIGHTS* in his neatest capital letters. Then he underlined it twice, just as Emily always did, only he couldn't find a ruler so he used the edge of the Jaffa Cake box. He sat back and admired his work. The underlining was a bit wobbly, and he'd been distracted by an awesome new Ferrari on *Top Gear* and had accidentally written LIGHGHGHTS, so he'd had to cross out the extra GHs. But apart from that, and a few smudges of chocolate, it didn't look bad at all.

He chewed the end of the pencil.

He doodled an epic battle between an alien and a goat in the corner of the page and multi-tasked by watching *Top Gear* until the adverts came on. He had a heading. Now he needed to add some notes. He remembered that Emily usually wrote down a list of witnesses to interview. He swept the biscuit crumbs off a new page and wrote WITLESS LIST. The problem was he was the only one who'd seen the lights. He wrote JACK CARTER. Then he crossed it out.

What was the point of interviewing himself?

Who else could have seen those lights? Jack wondered. He glanced at the telly as the *Top Gear* presenter welcomed the guest star onto the show. *Of course!* he thought. *Stars! Someone who's into stars might be looking at the sky in the middle of the night ...* And Jack knew just the person! He jumped off the sofa and ran upstairs to see if Scott wanted to go with him, but

Scott had a packed schedule of playing computer games all day. He called Emily, but she was being dragged off to Carrickstowe by her mum to buy a new school uniform.

So Jack went to interview Professor Atherton on his own.

Four

A Major Breakthrough

As he cycled to Coastguard Cottage to interview Professor Harry Atherton, Jack was feeling extraordinarily pleased with himself. The elderly scientist had helped the friends to identify a huge fossil they'd discovered at the old quarry last winter. It had turned out to be a new species of dinosaur – and one of their most exciting investigations ever!

But fossils weren't Professor Atherton's only interest.

He was also a keen astronomer. He'd had a glass observation dome built on top of the old watchtower at Coastguard Cottage, so that he could study the stars through his mega-powerful telescopes. If *anyone* on the island had witnessed the strange lights in the sky, Jack thought, it would be Professor Atherton.

Which is why, as he rang the doorbell, Jack was quite sure he'd have solved the mystery and have it all written up in his notebook before Emily even got back from the shops!

The door was opened by Professor Atherton's sister, Margaret, a small, lively woman with spiky grey hair. She was delighted to see Jack again and led him through the hall to the tower. It was just as Jack remembered: the circular walls filled with shelf after shelf of books, scientific specimens arranged in boxes or floating in jars, the huge mammoth skeleton and the strange lift that ran up the middle of the tower like a fireman's pole. Margaret shouted up to the gallery at the top for Professor Atherton to come down and join them.

'I've just made an apple pie,' Margaret said, showing Jack into the kitchen where she pushed a pile of books to the end of the table. 'Would you like some?'

Oh, yes, Jack thought as he tucked into a large slice, complete with vanilla ice cream, *this interview is going perfectly so far!* He was on his second helping when Professor Atherton coasted into the room. His electronic wheelchair bristled with more high-tech electronics than a cyborg from a science-fiction film. But beneath all the gadgets, he was an old man with a bushy beard, round glasses and a gruff voice. He was also paralysed from the neck down.

After chatting about the dinosaur fossil for a while, Jack explained the appearance of the phantom lights and asked if the professor had seen them.

Atherton pressed a button on the wheelchair's control pad with his chin and a huge computer screen shot out from the arm of the chair. He scrolled through calendars, maps and star charts. Jack wolfed down another piece of pie, trying to contain his excitement.

At last the professor spoke. 'Nothing!'

'Nothing?' Jack repeated, dropping his spoon.

'Not a sausage, I'm afraid. No moon that night and dense cloud cover. Very poor viewing conditions.'

Jack was so disappointed he almost forgot to thank Margaret Atherton as he got up to leave. If it hadn't been for her apple pie the whole trip would have been a total washout.

'It's funny you should mention those lights,' Margaret said, looking up from feeding her brother a piece of apple pie. 'I saw something like that the other night when I was driving home from Carrickstowe Hospital. Harry woke up with chest pains so I took him to get checked over. It turned out to be indigestion.' She gave her brother a stern look. 'Too much of my special vindaloo curry, I think!'

Atherton winked at Jack. 'My sister's always trying to bump me off by feeding me too much rich food.' Then he addressed Margaret. 'Let's have some more of that pie. Try not to get pastry crumbs all down my beard this time!'

Margaret ignored him and continued telling Jack her story. 'They kept Harry in hospital overnight. I was driving home when I saw what I thought was a pair of Search and Rescue helicopters hovering over the high moors. But now I think about it, I haven't heard of any incidents that would have called out the helicopters ...'

'What time was this?' Jack asked.

'Ooh, about two in the morning.'

Jack was so excited he sat back down and held his plate out for more pie and ice cream. 'That's exactly when I saw them too.'

'That can't be right!' Professor Atherton interrupted. 'You saw the lights the night before last?'

'Yes,' Jack said. 'Thursday night. We were on a glow-worm survey.'

'But that's *not* the night Margaret dragged me off to hospital.' Atherton nudged the control pad with his chin. The screen rotated so that Jack could see the calendar display. 'That was *Sunday* night. Four nights *before* your lights.'

Jack swallowed a mouthful of ice cream.

If the aliens had made *two* visits to Castle Key, chances were they'd be coming back for a third!

Back at Stone Cottage Jack called an emergency meeting in the tree house in the old chestnut tree in the back garden.

'Ughh,' Emily complained as she swung herself up from the ladder onto the platform and winched Drift up in his special basket. 'I hate clothes shopping.' Even though she'd changed back into her favourite cut-off denim shorts and old white t-shirt, the smell of itchy new school uniform still clung to her skin. 'So, what's this urgent and awesome information you texted us about?'

Jack made himself comfortable in the hammock that hung between two branches and pulled his rolled-up notebook out of his pocket. It kept furling itself up, so he bent the pages back. 'I've been conducting Operation Phantom Lights on my own,' he announced.

Emily frowned. She felt a little put out. If there was any investigating to be done around here, surely she should be in the know. And had Jack been *taking notes*? That was her job!

'Important Developments have developed,' Jack said in his most important voice.

'Like what?' Scott scoffed.

Jack told them about his brainwave of visiting Professor Atherton.

Emily couldn't help being impressed. 'Good idea! An astronomer would notice anything unusual in the night sky.'

'Exactly,' Jack said. 'Except he didn't.'

Scott rolled his eyes.

Jack took no notice. 'But Margaret did! Listen to this.' He cleared his throat and began to read from his notes:

'Miss Margaret Atherton observed strange flashing lights in the sky on Sunday 26th August at prosisely two o'clock in the morning. This offishly backs up all the details in the excellent account by the other ~~courajus corragius~~ brave witness (Jack Carter). This was four nights later. Same time and same place. So there, suckers!'

Scott looked over Jack's shoulder. 'You've spelled *precisely* wrong. And *officially*.'

'And you can't say *So there, suckers!* in a case report,' Emily objected.

'It's my report. I can say what I like.'

'So, what *are* you saying?' Scott asked. 'The aliens have a season ticket to Earth?'

Jack shrugged. 'I think they're looking for something. Which means they might come back again.'

Emily picked up Jack's notebook by one dog-eared corner as if it were a spider she'd found in her bath.

She scrunched up her nose at the Jaffa Cake smears and wobbly underlining, but then she nodded. 'Jack's right. This is a major breakthrough! If the lights were seen at two o'clock on both mornings in the same place, it suggests some kind of regular schedule – although I'm thinking of *human* activity rather than extraterrestrial.'

Emily dropped Jack's notebook back into his lap, pulled her own out of her bag and began to add the new information. 'Right,' she said, looking up at last. 'We need to keep watch to see if these lights come back again.'

'We?' Scott asked. 'I thought Jack had gone solo on this one. Count me out.'

'No way!' Emily cried. 'We're a team. We can't run an investigation without you! Can we?' she added, shooting Jack a look.

Jack was itching to wind Scott up by saying they could manage just fine without him, but he resisted the temptation. He supposed Scott did come in useful now and then; he was calm, logical, good at computer stuff and talking to old ladies. 'Yeah,' he said. 'We're like the Three Musketeers.'

Scott didn't show it – in case Jack took the credit – but he was thrilled that they had an investigation on the go again. Especially as his character in *Total Strategy* had just lost all his powers and was about to be exterminated by a horde of vampire zombies.

That night, Emily set her alarm for one in the morning. She leaped out of bed before it even rang – much to the surprise of Drift, who was curled up on her knees – grabbed her binoculars and ran to the window. Living on the eighth floor of a lighthouse definitely had its advantages! One of the three porthole windows faced north-west with a perfect view across Castle Key island towards the moors.

Emily gazed out into the night. The old stone tower of St Michael's was in her line of sight, and she watched the hands on the church clock go all the way round once, and then twice. Still no lights! At three o'clock she gave up and went back to bed.

The following night it was the boys' turn to keep watch. They climbed out of the window of their attic bedroom and perched on the slate roof that sloped gently down to the garden at the back of Stone Cottage for a better view.

But the only lights they saw were stars.

Scott voted that they abandon the whole sky-watching project. It was clearly a waste of time!

But Emily had other ideas. The next night was her turn again and all her sleuthing instincts told her that this was the night! She'd been looking at the calendar and had figured out a pattern: Jack saw the lights on Thursday night. Margaret Atherton had seen the lights on the Sunday before that, which was *four* nights earlier. What if the lights came back every fourth night?

It was now Monday, which was *four* nights since Jack's sighting ...

She couldn't sleep for excitement and began her watch at midnight. After an hour her eyelids were growing heavy ...

Suddenly, she heard the faint, mournful *bong!* of the church bell ringing the hour.

Bong! Bong!

Emily shook herself awake. *Two o'clock!* Had she missed it?

She snatched up her binoculars and peered into the dark.

In the distance, above the high ridge of the moor, she saw a flash.

Red then white then green.

The phantom lights were back!

Five

All Systems Go!

'Yes!' Emily breathed to Drift. 'It's all systems go!'

Drift didn't understand, of course, but he could sense her excitement so he wagged his tail to show his support.

Emily felt for the compass she'd placed ready on the windowsill. She held it up, rotated it until the arrow pointed in the precise direction of the flashing lights, read off the bearing of 310 degrees and jotted it down in her notebook. Then she just had time to snap a photograph of the lights before they disappeared.

Next, Emily ran to her desk. Using her school protractor, she measured fifty degrees from north on the map of Castle Key island she'd laid out ready, and drew a straight line at that angle, radiating from her position at The Lighthouse out across the moor. She had already drawn in a line that ran from their glow-worm campsite in the direction Jack had said he'd first seen the lights. Now they had two bearings and the point where the two lines crossed gave them a much more accurate idea of where the lights were located.

Emily stuffed the map and compass into her bag, pulled a black hooded sweatshirt on over her tracksuit and shoved her feet into her trainers. She'd planned this manoeuvre down to the last detail and now she ticked off each step as she put the plan into action.

Text to Jack and Scott telling them to meet her on the old quarry track – which was the quickest way to the moors. *Check!*

Night operations camouflage. Emily smeared stripes of dark face paint across her cheeks and forehead. *Check!*

Note for Mum and Dad. She'd probably be back before they even woke up and noticed she'd gone but, just in case, Emily had prepared a note saying she'd taken Drift out for a walk to leave on the blackboard in the kitchen on her way down. *Check!*

Now all she had to do was creep down the one hundred and twenty steps of the spiral staircase – carrying Drift so that his claws didn't make scratching noises on the wood – slip out of the door and jump on her bike. Then she'd pedal like crazy, meet the boys and together they'd race to the moors. Now they knew the exact position of the lights they might just find out what was going on – if they got to the scene fast enough.

She tiptoed across the landing and placed her foot on the first stair.

That's when she realized all the lights were on.

Emily leaned over the banister and looked down through the centre of the spiral staircase. Her mum was running up from the kitchen on the first floor. With her peacock-patterned dressing gown billowing and her dark curls flying out from a yellow silk scarf, she was flapping like a hummingbird.

'What's wrong?' Emily called.

'Come quickly!' Mum shouted. 'There's been an accident!'

As Emily flew down the stairs she remembered that Dad was away for the night visiting some old friends from his days as a guitarist in a rock band. Mum was an artist and she had an artistic temperament to go with it – which meant she was brilliant at creating dramas but hopeless at dealing with them.

She was in such a fluster she didn't even notice that Emily was fully dressed at two in the morning, let alone that she had black stripes on her face! 'It's Miss Wendover,' she wailed, as Emily joined her outside Guest Room Three. 'She's fallen over and hurt her ankle.'

Emily made it her business to carry out background checks on all the guests at The Lighthouse. You never knew when a seemingly innocent holidaymaker would turn out to be running an international crime ring. So she knew that Miss Millicent Wendover was eighty-two years old, that she'd been a policewoman most of her life and that she'd come to Castle Key to enjoy the scenery and take part in a pottery course at the Trago Gallery. No wonder Mum was freaking out; Miss Wendover was so frail she could easily have broken a bone.

Emily prised the pack of frozen peas from her mum's grasp and hurried into Miss Wendover's room. She helped the old lady onto the bed and placed a pink woollen cardigan around her shoulders. She wrapped the peas in a flannel and held them to the bump that was forming on the sparrow-sized ankle.

Miss Wendover smiled and said, 'Thank you, dear. Sorry to be such a fuss and bother!' But after half an hour the old lady was still shivering and her papery skin felt clammy. Emily found the first-aid kit in her shoulder bag, took out the thermometer and popped it into Miss Wendover's mouth.

The read-out said forty degrees.

Miss Wendover had a fever.

Emily handed the peas to her mum and phoned the out-of-hours medical service. The operator took some details and told her that Dr Armitage in Tregower was the doctor on call tonight and would be with them shortly. *That's lucky*, Emily thought, as she went down to the kitchen to make tea for everyone. Dr Armitage had been their family doctor for years. She would soon have everything under control.

When Emily opened the front door twenty minutes later she was surprised to find herself looking up at a man in a black leather jacket and designer jeans. He was young and tall and his beard was precision-trimmed to a line along his jaw. 'Sorry,' she said, realizing she was staring. 'I was expecting Dr Armitage.'

'Ah, yes! You have noticed that I am not a middle-aged white lady with sensible shoes, tweedy trousers and a no-nonsense hair-do? Your powers of observation are admirable!'

Emily smiled, feeling flattered, even though she knew the man was joking. She suddenly remembered the stripes of camo-paint on her face and tried to rub them off with her sleeve. She had a feeling the smudges weren't much of an improvement.

The man grinned and held out his hand. 'I'm Dr Mishra. I've stepped in to cover for Dr Armitage. It seems the switchboard weren't able to contact her.' He tapped on the motorbike helmet he was carrying under his arm. 'The bike's the quickest way to get out to these remote locations.'

After checking his ID card, Emily showed Dr Mishra to Miss Wendover's room. He soon confirmed that the old lady did indeed have a fever. 'She has flu. That's probably why she fell. Feeling a bit wobbly. The good news is that her ankle's fine. It's just bruised.' He gave Emily's mum a prescription for some medicine and told them to keep a close watch. 'Flu can be dangerous for the elderly,' he added. 'You were right to call.'

When the doctor had left Emily leaned against the front door and looked at her watch. It was almost half past three. So much for her every-second-counts plan to get to the moors in double-quick time. They might as well wait and go at first light now.

That's when she remembered she hadn't contacted the boys to cancel her text saying she would meet them. She checked her phone. Fifteen missed messages from Scott and Jack, each one grumpier than the last!

As they cycled along the track across the moors at six o'clock the next morning, Emily apologized for the gazillionth time for her no-show. The boys were distinctly unimpressed. After being woken by Emily's text at two in the morning, they'd hung about waiting for over an hour, before giving up and going back to bed.

'We couldn't even go and look by ourselves,' Scott grumbled, 'because you had the directions to where you saw the lights.'

But it was such a bright and sunny morning, with over-excited birds singing their heads off in the hedgerows and banks of wild flowers all competing to be the purplest of purples or the pinkest of pinks, it was impossible to stay cross for long.

Soon Jack was laughing as he freewheeled down a long hill. 'Emily's got a new crush!' he teased.

'What do you mean?' Emily demanded.

'Dr Mishra!' the boys chanted in chorus.

Emily almost wobbled off her bike. 'Do not!'

Scott laughed. 'You've said *Dr Mishra did this* and *Dr Mishra said that* about twenty times. You can't fool us!'

Emily refused to answer. She sped on in silence to the disused quarry where the track ended and they had to leave their bikes and continue on foot. She consulted her map, on which she'd plotted the compass bearings. Then she pointed across the moor. 'We need to head in this direction for half a kilometre, cross the stream and bear ten degrees north-west!' she snapped.

With that, Emily set off at a brisk stomp without looking back. Drift hopped down from the bike basket and trotted after her.

The boys exchanged grins. Then they followed. But they hadn't gone far when Scott realized that *they* were being followed too ...

Six

A Strange Disappearance

Scott nudged Jack's elbow. 'Don't look now, but I can hear footsteps behind us.'

Jack turned round. Scott grabbed his arm. 'I said *don't* look!'

'You're imagining things,' Jack said.

But then he heard it too.

He stopped. So did the noise.

He glanced over his shoulder. There was no one there.

Who else would be wandering around the moors at the crack of dawn anyway? Jack wondered. They weren't even on a path. They were striking out across steep, rough terrain, clambering over boulders and weaving between gorse thickets.

Then he heard the noise again.

This is getting seriously creepy, Jack thought. It was just like when that goat had sneaked up on him the night he saw the phantom lights. And now he'd got Dotty's spooky stories about evil pixies luring unsuspecting travellers into perilous swamps going round in his head too, not to mention restless spirits rising up from burial grounds, stranded aliens and the wandering ghosts of World War Two pilots. *Let's face it*, he thought, *these moors are* swarming *with hazardous paranormal activity!*

Even in broad daylight it was enough to give a guy the collywobbles!

Jack couldn't stand the suspense any longer. He knelt and pretended to be tying the laces on his trainers. As soon as heard the noise again he whipped round.

This time he caught a flash of purple disappearing behind a gorse bush. He torpedoed down the hill and launched himself over the bush. He landed smack-bang on top of the sinister stalker-beast and pinned it to the ground.

To Jack's total and utter horror, it was a *girl*!

A punching, kicking, karate-chopping girl!

'Ouch! Ahh! Oomph!' Jack cried, flying backwards as if he'd been electrocuted. He landed with a *thwump* in a clump of bracken.

Scott came running down the slope, followed by Emily and Drift.

Emily stared down at the girl, who was sitting up brushing grass off her purple t-shirt and white jeans. 'Rosie?'

Scott looked at Emily in surprise. 'You know her?'

'It's Rosie Armitage. She's in the year above me at school. But why was Jack attacking her?'

'I wasn't *attacking* her!' Jack spluttered. 'It was self-defence. I thought she was a goat or a pixie or an alien ...' His voice trailed off as he realized he wasn't doing himself any favours.

'Thanks very much!' Rosie laughed.

Scott grinned. 'My brother's a real smooth-talker with girls.'

Jack went so red his face could have stopped traffic. He wished Rosie *had* been a pixie goat-beast from outer space. She might have ripped his head off or shoved him into a swamp, but at least he wouldn't be dying of embarrassment.

'You've got some good defensive moves there,' Scott told Rosie.

Rosie smiled. 'Thanks. I'm a green belt in karate.'

'What are you doing up here?' Emily asked, sitting down on the grass.

'And why were you stalking us?' Jack added.

'I'm looking for my gran. She's disappeared,' Rosie said, raking twigs from her long brown hair with her fingers and re-tying her ponytail. She turned to Jack and Scott. 'I'm sorry about sneaking up on you. I didn't see Emily and Drift at first, just two strange boys I didn't recognize. You were acting a bit suspiciously, heading off into the middle of the moors, so I thought you might have something to do with Gran going missing.'

Scott sat down next to Emily and Rosie. 'Disappeared? How do you mean?'

'She went off in the middle of the night with a man on a motorbike.'

Scott stared at her. 'What would she do that for?'

'Gran's a doctor,' Rosie explained. 'This man came knocking on our door. Mum and I have lived with my gran since Dad left,' she added. 'This man said there'd been an accident on the moor and he begged her to come quickly.'

'Weren't you asleep if it was the middle of the night?' Jack asked, taking a Coke out of his backpack and handing it to Rosie as a peace offering – even if she *had* karate-chopped him *and* called him a strange boy *and* accused him of stealing people's grandmothers. 'Sorry I pounced on you,' he mumbled.

'Don't mention it!' Rosie opened the can and quickly held it at arm's length as it sprayed shaken-up Coke all over her.

'I was reading this amazing book,' Rosie said, going back to Jack's question. '*The Moonrise Dragons*. I was meant to have turned my light off but I was reading under the duvet. You know what it's like when you just *have* to finish a book?'

'Er, yeah, it's a killer,' Jack fibbed. 'Happens to me all the time.'

Rosie gazed out across the rugged landscape as she continued. 'I heard the motorbike stop outside and a knock at the front door. I looked out of the window and saw this guy talking to Gran. All I could hear was something about an accident on the high moor. Gran was on call last night so her medical bag was ready by the door. She grabbed it, ran out and jumped on the back of the motorbike and they zoomed off.' Rosie paused and chewed her lip. 'I haven't seen her since.'

As Rosie spoke, Scott noticed that Emily had gone quiet. Normally she'd have switched into hyper-drive at the first hint of a missing person. 'Are you alright?' he asked.

Emily didn't reply. She *wasn't* alright. Ever since Rosie had mentioned the man on the motorbike she'd felt as if iced water were trickling down her spine, drop by chilling drop. 'What time did all this happen?' she asked.

'About half past two in the morning,' Rosie said.

Emily swallowed hard. The pieces were falling into place so fast she could practically feel the G-force. 'Your gran is Dr Armitage, isn't she?'

Rosie made a puzzled face. 'Yeah, of course she is. You know that. She's your doctor. You've been to her surgery in Tregower. We live right next door to it.'

Emily got to her feet, took a step or two and stared into the distance. At last she spoke. 'Last night, at about half past two, I called for a doctor to come and see one of the guests at The Lighthouse. Shortly after that a man turned up ... on a motorbike!' Emily's voice dropped almost to a whisper as she turned back to face Rosie and the boys. 'He *said* he was the doctor covering for your gran because the switchboard couldn't contact her!'

Rosie gasped, her hazel eyes almost popping out of her head. 'That must have been the man who took her!'

'Dr Mishra!' Scott and Jack cried in unison.

Emily nodded slowly. She felt sick. How could she have been fooled? Dr Mishra – if that was even his real name – had seemed so friendly, and yet, just moments before he'd called at The Lighthouse, he'd abducted Dr Armitage! He was an imposter, a kidnapper, maybe even a *murderer*! His ID card must have been a fake.

But Rosie giggled. 'Dr Mishra? No way! It wasn't him.'

'Are you sure?' Scott asked.

'Sure I'm sure! Dr Mishra is a friend of Gran's. I've met him lots of times. The man I saw last night was much shorter. I didn't get a very good look at him, but

54

he had a beard. It was a pale colour – blond or light brown.'

Emily sank down on to the grass. She felt a bit silly for suspecting the doctor. 'Obviously, I was just checking so we can eliminate Dr Mishra from our enquiries!'

'Enquiries?' Rosie repeated. 'Does that mean you'll help me look for Gran?'

Scott, Jack and Emily all nodded. Drift wagged his tail and licked Rosie's hand as if to agree.

As she thanked them, Rosie's eyes welled with tears. 'Mum's in bed with flu so she's no help and, anyway, she says Gran's probably just been called in to help out at the hospital or something.' Rosie took her phone from her pocket and checked it. 'But Gran *still* hasn't replied to my texts. I know there's something wrong.' Suddenly she frowned. 'So that's why *I'm* up here, but how come you three are out on the moors so early in the morning?'

Emily hesitated. Should they let Rosie in on Operation Phantom Lights? Rosie seemed reliable enough: a quiet, dreamy girl, not the sort to reveal classified information to enemies, but you could never be too careful. But before Emily could decide, Jack was already spilling the whole story, inter-galactic goat abductions and all.

Scott glared at him. '*Jack* may be looking for aliens, but Emily and I are simply investigating some unexplained lights.'

'Exactly,' Emily said. 'We've pinpointed the likely

location from compass bearings and we're on our way there now. We can join forces and look for your gran at the same time. You're on the team – as long as you promise not to reveal the nature of our operations to anyone, even if you are captured by enemy forces and tortured.'

Rosie nodded solemnly. 'I promise.'

Seven

Suspicious Behaviour

The friends soon found the spot Emily had marked on the map from her compass bearings. It was a flat stony area further up the slope from the ravine where they'd previously found the plane wreckage, the morning after Jack saw the phantom lights.

They searched and searched but there was nothing to be seen apart from the herd of grazing goats wandering by. Jack was convinced that the black and white one he'd seen on the night of the phantom lights was still missing from the herd. Scott refused to believe Jack could tell one goat from another. They were still arguing the point when Emily spotted a faint footprint on a dusty rock. She checked it against her photos of the prints she'd found near the ravine on their last visit. It matched perfectly! Suddenly Emily thought of something.

'What size are your gran's feet?' she asked Rosie.

Rosie was checking under a thick gorse bush. 'Six and a half, I think.' She looked at Scott, Jack and Emily. 'Why've you all gone quiet?'

Emily pointed at the print on the rock. 'Does she have a pair of shoes with soles like this?'

Rose shrugged. 'I don't know. I've never checked the bottoms of her shoes. Is it important?'

'It's just that we spotted some size six and a half footprints like this ...' Emily began.

'Yeah, right by the edge of that massive great ravine down there!' Jack added.

Rosie's hands flew to her mouth. She began to run down the slope.

By the time Scott, Jack and Emily caught up with her, Rosie was kneeling at the edge of the ravine, yelling, 'Gran! Can you hear me?'

It took all the friends' efforts to convince Rosie that Dr Armitage hadn't plunged into the ravine. 'If Jack had let Emily finish her sentence,' Scott explained, shooting Jack an accusing look, 'she was going to say that we found those footprints last Friday. The morning after Jack first saw the phantom lights. That's four days ago!'

'Long before your gran disappeared last night!' Emily added.

Rosie laughed with relief. Then she laughed again as Drift nudged her elbow with his nose as if trying to push her away from the edge of the ravine. He backed away on his belly, howling softly.

'Don't worry!' Jack told Rosie. 'Drift's just doing his voodoo freak-out routine again. This place is haunted.'

Rosie gulped. 'Let's go and search somewhere else,' she said quickly.

—

By the time they took a break to eat the picnic lunch that Jack had so brilliantly thought to pack in his rucksack, they were all wilting in the midday heat. They walked to the bottom of the valley, took off their shoes and waded out into the shallow stream to sit on the flat rocks that rose up like giant stepping stones. Drift splashed about, gleefully chasing the tiny fish that darted through the clear water. The others were less cheerful. They were still no closer to finding Dr Armitage or the cause of the phantom lights.

Jack dangled his feet in the icy water as he munched his way through ham sandwiches, pickled onion crisps and a slab of Aunt Kate's carrot cake. He had his own theory about what had happened to Dr Armitage. She must have encountered the aliens when she'd come up to the moors with Motorbike Man to attend to an accident. They'd zapped her up to their spaceship, where she was probably now wired up to bizarre brain-scrambling electrodes. He kept this scenario to himself though: one, because he didn't want to upset Rosie (any more than he already had done) and, two, because Scott and Emily rolled their eyes every time he even thought the word *alien*.

Suddenly Jack noticed something glinting among the smooth brown pebbles under the water. He reached in and picked up a small silver key. The number forty-two was engraved on one side and the peculiar words *De Gele Tulp* on the other. He held it out to show the others.

'That key could have been in the stream for years,' Scott pointed out. 'Anyone could have dropped it. Probably just a tourist out on a hike.'

But Emily was sure the key was an important clue. She dried it and sealed it in an evidence pouch and popped it into her bag.

They continued the search through the afternoon. Finally, when the light began to fade, they gave up and agreed to start again the next day. Rosie headed back to Tregower, while Emily, Scott, Jack and Drift returned to the abandoned quarry, where they'd left their bikes propped against one of the derelict stone buildings.

Jack was looking forward to getting home to a massive plate of pasta, followed by the dream combination of sofa, telly and ice cream.

But then he spotted a man with a beard.

Jack dived behind one of the crumbling stone walls that dotted the old quarry works, pulling Scott and Emily with him. Drift bounced after them, wondering if this was a new game.

Jack peeped out. It was twilight now. The abandoned buildings loomed out of the shadows, the black holes of caved-in doors and windows gaping like open mouths and vacant eyes. The silence was eerie, as if the place were haunted by the workers who'd once toiled here. Jack could almost hear the clang of pickaxes and hammers against the stone. Behind the tall wire fence that closed off the old quarry pits, he could make out the white tent that covered the site of the dinosaur fossil they'd found there last winter. During the day, scientists would be busy with the delicate work of excavating the fossil, but now, at dusk, the site was deserted.

Deserted, that was, except for a skinny man with a straggly brown beard scurrying towards the overgrown opening of an old tunnel.

Jack did a double take.

It was Don Penrose!

Why was the leader of Castle Key Nature Group skulking around the disused quarry? And why was he carrying an electronic gadget that looked like a brick-sized mobile phone from a 1980s movie?

'He's communicating with the aliens!' Jack breathed.

'He's kidnapped Dr Armitage!' Emily whispered.

Scott didn't say a word. In fact, he was trying not to laugh. Don Penrose was so mild-mannered he wouldn't step on an ant. Scott couldn't decide which was less likely – Jack's notion that Don was secretly co-ordinating an alien invasion or Emily's idea that he was a kidnapper of old ladies! *And yet*, Scott found himself thinking. *And yet* … Don *had* been there on the night that Jack first saw the phantom lights. Could the glow-worm camp have been a cover story for a nocturnal meeting with alien visitors? And he *did* fit Rosie's description of the bearded man who'd whisked her gran away on his motorbike.

And right now, on a scale of one to ten of suspicious behaviour, Don Penrose was scoring eleven! He was creeping towards an old tunnel, glancing over his shoulder every few seconds. He was also twiddling knobs on the electronic device, which was making beeping and squelching sounds.

Scott couldn't help looking up at the stars twinkling in the darkening sky. Was Penrose talking to someone up there?

Emily could hardly believe it either. *Don Penrose was a criminal!* It was like catching Santa sneaking down the chimney and stealing all the presents from under the tree! But, she reminded herself, *a good investigator is never fooled by appearances*. Don's herbal tea and digestive biscuits, his socks and sandals and his *Save the Whales* t-shirt, could all be a cleverly constructed disguise for his underhand activities.

Suddenly Don Penrose gave a startled cry. Emily closed her eyes and groaned. She hadn't noticed Drift trotting out to greet him with a friendly nudge to the back of his knees. Of course, Drift wasn't to know that their friend was now their prime suspect!

Don laughed nervously as he recognized Drift and crouched down to ruffle his fur. 'You gave me a fright there, old boy!' He stood up and looked around, knowing that Emily couldn't be far away.

Emily grimaced at the boys.

They had little choice but to show themselves and act normal.

Eight

One Big Mystery

Emily, Scott and Jack stepped out from behind the wall.

'Oh, hi there, Don,' Emily chirped as if she'd just noticed him. 'We were just, er ...'

'Looking for some more glow-worms,' Jack chipped in.

'Super! Super!' Don said. 'I wish all the young people in the Nature Group were as keen as you three!'

'So, are you up here looking for glow-worms too?' Scott asked, trying to sound casual.

'No, not glow-worms. I'm looking for something else …' Don tugged at his untidy beard and glanced around as if worried they might be overheard. 'Actually, I'd appreciate it if you didn't mention you'd seen me here …'

Now Emily *knew* she was right! Don was obviously arranging to meet his fellow kidnappers to discuss their plans for Dr Armitage. *He's got a nerve to think that we'll cover up for him*, she thought, *but we'll have to play along until we know what's going on.* 'Don't worry, we won't give you away,' she said with her fingers crossed behind her back. She directed her gaze to the electronic device. 'So, you're using the radio to make contact?'

'Oh, no, this isn't a radio,' Don said. 'It's for picking up signals that our human ears can't detect.'

'You mean, the *aliens*?' Jack croaked. He was so filled with a mixture of excitement and I-told-you-so smugness that he could hardly speak.

Don looked bemused for a moment. Then he smiled. 'No, they're a native species actually. You must be thinking of squirrels.'

Now it was Jack's turn to look baffled. He was thinking of many things but *squirrels* definitely wasn't one of them.

'Grey squirrels?' Don prompted. 'They're an alien

species to Britain. They've invaded and pushed out the native red squirrels in many areas. It's quite a problem.'

Drift began to run around excitedly; *squirrels* was one of his favourite words. Then he flopped down in disappointment. Why did people keep saying *squirrels* when there clearly weren't any around? There weren't even any trees here!

'So what *are* you looking for?' Scott asked, trying to get the conversation back under control. It was getting more random by the second!

'Barbastelles.'

'Barbastelles?' Scott, Jack and Emily echoed in unison.

'Bats,' Don explained. 'They're an extremely rare species. I'm pretty sure there are some roosting in here.' He pointed to the tunnel mouth behind him, half-obscured by a veil of brambles. He held up the device. 'This is a bat detector. It picks up their ultrasonic calls – which are too high for us to hear – so that then you can play them back at a lower frequency. Listen!' He pressed a button and a series of clicks and warbles came out. Don's face lit up. 'Absolutely super, isn't it?'

'Super,' Emily murmured weakly.

'But if you're just looking for bats,' Scott asked, 'why didn't you want anyone to know you're here?'

Don puffed out his cheeks. 'I applied to the owners of the quarry site for permission to do a bat survey, but it was turned down on health and safety grounds.

Apparently the tunnel is dangerous. They want me to wait until they've strengthened it, but that work might disturb the bats! If I can prove the bats are here then they'll have to be more careful to protect the barbastelles while they carry out any work.' He paused. 'You're welcome to stay and help me with the recordings. I've got some biscuits and a flask.'

Jack had to admit that spending the night in a dark tunnel listening to bat calls did sound cool in a spooky kind of way, but he was tired and hungry. He wasn't sure he'd survive on a quarter-share of Don's digestive biscuits and lukewarm tea. Along with Emily and Scott, he politely declined the offer and headed home.

—

That evening Emily and her parents sat down to a late dinner in the kitchen. Dad was back from seeing his friends, full of plans for a big reunion gig with his old band, Panic Mode. Mum was all abuzz too, because an important art gallery in St Ives was interested in exhibiting some of her paintings. Emily was pleased for them both but was soon bored. Why couldn't her parents ever talk about anything interesting, like crimes and clues and suspects? She slipped away and called in to see Miss Wendover, who was sitting up in bed feeling much better.

This is more like it! Emily thought, as the old lady

enthralled her with police stories, from her early days as a uniformed officer after World War Two to her years in the Criminal Investigations Department.

Emily even told Miss Wendover about the phantom lights and the search for Dr Armitage. She didn't normally give away operational information, of course, but she figured this didn't count, since the old lady was a fellow professional crime-fighter.

Miss Wendover clasped her hands together beneath her chin. 'Hmm. I'd be very surprised if those strange lights and your disappearing doctor weren't connected in some way.' The old lady paused and chuckled. 'The tricky part is to find the link between them, of course! What do you have to go on so far?'

'Not much,' Emily admitted. She held out the key Jack had found in the stream. 'We found this on the moor.'

'*De Gele Tulp*?' Miss Wendover said, examining the key through the magnifying glass Emily passed to her. 'That's Dutch. It means *The Yellow Tulip*.' She looked up at Emily over her half-moon glasses. 'I picked up the language when I was undercover in Amsterdam in the 1970s, tracking down a major gun-running gang.'

Emily gazed at Miss Wendover in admiration. That sounded like her idea of heaven! 'It says forty-two on the other side,' she said. 'Could it be a hotel room key?'

Miss Wendover nodded. 'Holland is famous for tulips. There are lots of hotels and inns named after them.' She leaned back against her pillows and closed her eyes.

Emily was about to ask more questions when she realized the old lady was fast asleep.

Emily settled down on her bed to write up the day's events in her notebook. Not that there was much to add. Operation Phantom Lights wasn't exactly progressing at breakneck speed. They still had no idea what had caused the strange lights.

She turned to a fresh page and wrote *OPERATION DISAPPEARING DOCTOR*. Then she summarized Rosie's account of her gran vanishing into the night with the man on the motorbike. They weren't having any success with this case either. She laughed out loud to think they'd suspected Don Penrose of kidnap. Now she'd got over the disappointment of losing her prime suspect, Emily was glad their friend was guilty of nothing more than being batty about bats!

Which just left some unidentified size six and a half footprints and a key for a hotel room somewhere in Holland. After tiptoeing out of Miss Wendover's room, Emily had gone straight to the computer in the family living room and looked up *The Yellow Tulip* on the internet. There were over thirty hotels of that name in Holland, but even if she could somehow find out *which* of those hotels the key came from, she wasn't sure how it would help.

Now we have two investigations going nowhere fast, she thought.

Or did they? What if the strange lights and the missing doctor were part of one big mystery? And was the connection between them the key to solving the case, as Miss Wendover seemed to think?

But surely Rosie's gran is just an ordinary country doctor? Emily thought. *Unless, of course, she's secretly leading a double life …* 'I think we need to find out a bit more about Dr Armitage,' Emily told Drift as she turned out the light. 'Maybe she's an undercover agent for MI5, or part of an organized crime ring.'

Drift was curled up at the end of the bed. He perked up one ear, but there was really only one question on *his* mind: what had happened to those squirrels he'd been promised?

Nine

Danger at the Ravine

When Emily and Drift called at Stone Cottage the next morning, they found Scott and Jack eating breakfast in the kitchen. Aunt Kate set another place for Emily while Drift took up position under the table. Aunt Kate's tabby kitten, Boomerang, shot him a warning glare to let him know that she was first in line for scraps.

While Aunt Kate was busy frying bacon and eggs

Emily quickly told the boys about Miss Wendover's suggestion that Dr Armitage's disappearance was connected to the phantom lights. 'So we need to check out whether there is anything shady in Dr Armitage's past,' she concluded.

Before Emily had even finished speaking Scott had a great idea. Aunt Kate had lived in Castle Key for years and, although she kept it extremely hush-hush, she had once worked for the secret service – as the friends had discovered during Operation Skylark last year. She might well have some useful background intelligence. 'Aunt Kate, do you happen to know Dr Armitage?' he asked casually.

Aunt Kate turned round from the old-fashioned range cooker and wiped her hands on her blue-striped apron. 'Yes, of course! Lucinda Armitage is an old friend. And,' she added, looking over her glasses, 'sorry to disappoint you, but she is not a secret agent or a Mafia boss!'

Scott grinned. He should have realized that with her spy training Aunt Kate had been tuning in to their conversation over the sizzling of the bacon! But he couldn't help feeling disappointed, even though Emily's Dr-Armitage-has-a-secret-life theory had always been a long shot.

Aunt Kate shared the rinds out between Drift and Boomerang. 'But now I think about it, Lucinda did do some high-security research for the Ministry of Defence a few years back.'

The three friends looked at each other. *High security! Ministry of Defence!* These were exactly the kind of words they'd been longing to hear!

'She was part of a team studying the medical effects of radiation,' Aunt Kate explained. 'You know, fallout from accidents at nuclear power stations, or even nuclear weapons. I don't know the details, of course ...'

Jack continued to thump ketchup all over his plate, but Scott and Emily were too busy thinking about nuclear radiation to eat.

Along with bacon and eggs, had Aunt Kate just served up the clue that would blow the case wide open?

—

An hour later the friends were cycling towards the old quarry where they'd arranged to meet Rosie Armitage. As they pedalled along the track, they discussed Aunt Kate's intriguing information.

Scott had a theory.

'A nuclear bomb?' Jack laughed. 'In Castle Key? I think we'd have noticed!'

'I didn't say a *bomb*!' Scott snapped. 'I said, what if there are people doing some kind of secret nuclear testing in an underground laboratory beneath the moors? Dr Armitage could have found out about it and been about to tell the world how dangerous it is.'

'Of course,' Emily said. 'They kidnapped her to stop her going public.'

'And it would explain the strange lights too,' Scott went on. 'They could be part of the testing – explosions and stuff.'

Jack felt his skin prickle. If Scott was right, they could be covered in radioactive particles already. He didn't know exactly what radiation looked like or what it did, but he was pretty sure it wasn't good for you. He scratched his bare arms. It was like head lice: you could feel them crawling all over your scalp as soon as anyone started talking about them.

'And I've got a hunch as to where that secret laboratory might be,' Scott was saying. 'Think about it! Why does Drift always act so weird at the ravine? Maybe it's not really ghosts from that old plane crash spooking him out. Maybe he can sense the radioactivity fizzing about in the air.' Scott stood up on the pedals of his bike and put on a spurt of speed. 'I bet the entrance to the underground lab is in the ravine!'

Rosie was already waiting near the old quarry when the friends arrived. She struck a lonely figure, sitting on a stone wall with her shoulders hunched and her elbows on her knees, her long hair draped over her face. 'Gran's still missing,' she reported as she jumped down from the wall.

Emily gave her a hug. 'Has your mum called the police yet?'

Rosie shook her head. 'She got a text message last night from Gran's phone. It said *Having a few days' break. Back soon.* Mum says it proves Gran's fine, but she's feeling so grotty with the flu she's not thinking straight. Gran wouldn't just go off on holiday without telling us.' Rosie paused and sighed. 'I'm sure Gran's kidnapper forced her to write that message so that nobody would come looking for her.'

Emily nodded wisely. 'You're right. That is a classic kidnappers' move.'

'And I checked out which shoes Gran was wearing when she disappeared,' Rosie said. 'Just to see if they matched those prints you found by the ravine.' She handed Emily a print-out of a photo of a flat, beige ankle boot turned over to show the sole. 'She has two pairs like this. They're her favourites,' Rosie explained. 'One pair is missing so she must be wearing them.'

Emily, Scott and Jack all looked at the photo. It was clear the boots didn't match the footprints they'd seen. The soles were patterned with circles, not crosses.

'I know you didn't think she'd fallen in the ravine anyway,' Rosie said, 'because you found the footprints days ago. But I wanted to be sure, just in case she'd been there earlier and then gone back again ...'

Emily smiled. 'Excellent work! A good investigator always checks every detail.'

Rosie sighed. 'I just wish it helped us find Gran.'

Jack patted Rosie's arm kindly – although rather nervously in case she karate-chopped him again. 'Don't worry. We've figured it all out. Your gran's been nabbed by some mad scientists with a nuclear bomb.'

Rosie's eyes widened in horror. 'Is that meant to make me feel *better*?'

Scott glared at Jack. 'Not helping!' he mouthed.

Jack groaned to himself. Ever since he'd got off to that bad start with Rosie by pouncing on her, he'd been trying his best to make up for it. But the more he tried to be nice, the more he put his foot in it! He listened gloomily while Scott explained his theory about the nuclear testing lab to Rosie.

'Which is why,' Scott said in conclusion, 'we need to go back to the ravine and find the concealed entrance.'

'OK,' Rosie said seriously. 'Let's do it.'

Just for once, Jack thought, *I wish it could be Scott who made a total goon of himself instead of me!*

—

Scott, Jack, Emily and Rosie stood in a row staring down into the ravine. It looked exactly the same as the day before, except that there had been a shower in the night, so the stony ground was wet. The size six and a half footprints had all washed away. There had been some mudslides along the sides of the ravine and steam was rising gently from the rusty wing of the wrecked aeroplane as raindrops evaporated in the morning sun.

Scott looked over the edge. He was sure there must be a tunnel or a door hidden somewhere in the ravine. Drift was whimpering and pawing at the ground behind him as he inched closer for a better view.

Suddenly Scott slipped. His feet shot out in front of him and he landed with a thud in the mud on the seat of his jeans. Before he could pull back from the edge, the ground began to fall away beneath him. He scrabbled with his hands. He tried to dig in with his heels. But it was no good. He was flying down the wall of the ravine as if on a runaway sledge, but with no soft snow to cushion his fall. Sharp stones jabbed and stabbed at him. He bounced off a rock, tumbling over and over now, picking up speed.

Scott closed his eyes and clenched his teeth, bracing for impact.

He knew the bottom of the ravine was strewn with jagged rocks and twisted metal.

Suddenly the falling stopped. Scott felt the air knocked out of him. It was like running into a brick wall at full tilt.

Not daring to move, Scott opened his eyes. He was lying on his front, straddling the trunk of a small hawthorn tree that had somehow managed to take root and grow out from the near-vertical wall of the ravine. It was the scrawniest, weediest tree he'd ever seen, but it had broken his fall.

At the top of the ravine, Jack, Emily and Rosie stood with their mouths hanging open in shock. One second Scott was right there. The next he was gone!

Jack dropped to his knees, clutching his head in his hands. This was all his fault. He had wished that Scott would make a goon of himself and now he had – only it had all gone horribly wrong ...

Ten

Drift Takes Charge

Jack peeped out through his fingers. He could hardly bring himself to look down into the void. But suddenly he jumped to his feet, shouting and laughing. 'Scott's OK! He's stuck on a tree!'

Emily and Rosie looked over the edge to see for themselves.

'Hang on!' Emily shouted. 'We'll get you out of there!'

'I'll call Mountain Rescue,' Rosie said, reaching for her phone.

'Hurry up!' came a cry from the deep. 'This tree's about to give way!'

'There's no time for Mountain Rescue,' Jack cried, starting to lower himself over the edge. 'I'll climb down.'

'No way!' Emily and Rosie yelled, grabbing him by the arms. 'It's too dangerous,' Emily snapped. 'Look how the wall's crumbling. We need to think!'

Jack struggled against the girls' grip. Scott may be an infuriating know-it-all, but he was the best big brother he had, and he was hanging onto a twig halfway down a bottomless pit full of nuclear bombs. There was no time to waste *thinking*! 'Ropes!' he yelled. 'I need some ropes!'

Emily dug in her bag. All she found was a big ball of parcel string.

Jack snorted. 'That won't hold Scott's weight!'

'I know!' Rosie cried. 'We can plait loads of strands together to make a stronger rope!'

'Brilliant!' Emily grabbed the scissors from her bag and began cutting the string into long lengths.

'I got the idea from a book,' Rosie said, as they began plaiting the strands so fast their fingers were a blur.

Emily was puzzled. She'd read the *Survival Guide for Secret Agents* a hundred times, but she'd never come across this tip. Was there a better survival book out there that she'd missed? 'What book?' she asked.

'*The Moonrise Dragons*,' Rosie said. 'The one I was telling you about. Princess Leylana has to rescue her cousin Krimon from ...' Rosie's voice tailed off as she realized this was not the best time to tell the whole story. Jack was pacing up and down threatening to leap over the edge if they didn't get a move on. 'Well, anyway,' Rosie added, 'Leylana actually cuts off her long golden hair and uses that to weave the rope, but I thought it might work with string.'

'Is that rope long enough yet?' Jack shouted.

'Not quite,' Emily told him. 'We're going as fast as we can.'

'I can't hold on much longer!' Scott yelled from below.

—

Meanwhile, Drift was so anxious he thought his ears were about to explode.

He'd tried and tried to warn the humans about the crumbling edges of the ravine, but they hadn't listened. Now Scott had fallen in! Drift could smell Emily, Jack and Rosie's panic, and hear it in their voices, but why weren't they climbing down to get him out?

Drift knew he had to take charge.

He ran to the end of the ravine and squeezed through a gap not much bigger than a rabbit hole. In fact, he'd thought it *was* a rabbit hole when he'd found it yesterday,

83

which is why he'd stuck his nose down it. It had turned out to be a tiny steep tunnel carved out by a trickle of a waterfall. He'd not gone all the way to the end as he'd been afraid he might get stuck, but he was sure it would come out eventually at the bottom of the ravine.

Today, getting stuck was a risk he was going to have to take.

Drift scrabbled at the earth with his paws like a mole and tore at roots with his teeth. He scrabbled and tore, tore and scrabbled, until at last he popped out into the ravine. His paws burning, he picked his way across the rocks and wreckage until he could see Scott hanging from the tree above him. He'd planned to scramble up the wall of the ravine, but to his dismay he could see now that it was too steep. He gave a soft bark of encouragement and began to search around for some other way to help Scott.

He came across some bones and gave them a quick sniff. They were pretty old. *Human! That's unusual*, he thought, but there was no time to investigate further. He could hear that scrawny hawthorn tree creaking from here. Then he picked up another human scent. It was very faint and mixed up with rotten canvas and mouse droppings. At last he traced it to a brown bag with ropes spilling out of it.

Suddenly Drift knew what he had to do. He'd seen Jack climb down a steep rock face using ropes like these before ...

He grabbed the canvas bag between his teeth and began to drag it towards the tunnel. Getting back up would be twice as hard as coming down but somehow he would do it!

—

'It's still not long enough!' Jack yelled as Rosie and Emily lowered their rope of plaited string over the side of the ravine. 'I'll have to go down without it. Scott's going to fall any minute.' He was about to launch himself over the edge when he heard a panting noise. He looked round to see Drift staggering towards him, dragging what looked like a canvas sack. The courageous canine made it as far as Jack's feet, where he collapsed, his long pink tongue hanging from his jaws and his sides heaving.

Emily knelt and hugged Drift. Then she poured water from a bottle into her hands for him to lick at. 'Poor thing! You're exhausted. Where've you been?'

'This bag's got ropes in it!' Jack shouted. 'Drift, you're a *legend*! Em, Rosie! Quick! Help me get them out.'

As the friends tugged the tangled ropes from the bag, they found they were attached to swathes of folded cloth. 'It's an old parachute,' Rosie said. 'It must have belonged to the war plane that crashed.'

Within minutes, Jack had cut the ropes free of the parachute and tied lengths together using his best rock-climbing knots. Emily found an old tent peg in her bag and hammered it into the ground with a rock to serve as an anchor. Jack tied one end of the rope to it and lowered the other end – with the parachute harness still attached – over the side.

Down in the ravine, Scott caught hold of the rope and buckled the straps of the harness across his chest. He had no idea where the others had managed to find an old parachute, but he'd never been so relieved to see anything in his life! As he tugged on the rope to tell them he was ready, the hawthorn tree cracked in two.

With a combination of Scott climbing, and the other three hauling him up, he was soon almost at the top. He was looking forward to having his feet back on solid ground when he caught a glimpse of a bag hanging from beneath the wing of the crashed plane. The wing hid the bag from view from the top of the ravine. For a moment, Scott thought it must be a pilot's kit bag that had fallen from inside the plane. But then he noticed something that made his heart go into overdrive again. 'Stop a minute!' he shouted to the rope-heavers at the top. 'I can see something …'

'You'll see the bottom of the ravine if we don't get you up fast!' Jack hollered back. 'This edge is crumbling.'

Then came Emily's voice. 'What can you see?'

'A bag. It's hanging under the wing.'

'So what?' Jack yelled. 'It's just part of the plane wreck.'

'It's blue and shiny and it's got a Nike logo on the side,' Scott shouted.

There was a silence as the three friends at the top of the ravine processed this information. 'You mean it's a *new* bag?' Emily called down.

'Looks like it!'

'How did it get there?' Rosie called.

'That's what I want to know!' Scott yelled back.

He looked up and saw a plaited white string snaking down the rocks towards him. On the end was a hook, fashioned from wire, and a weight made from a penknife. He grabbed the string and tied one end to his harness. Then he threw the other end towards the bag. It was difficult to get a good aim while dangling from the rope but at the fifth attempt he made it. The hook snagged the handle of the bag and he was able to pull it free from the metal strut it was caught on. There was a touch-and-go moment as the bag – which was surprisingly heavy – fell and swung on the end of the string, almost pulling Scott down with it. But he held it fast and hauled it up like a giant fish on the end of a line.

At last Scott was crawling up over the lip of the ravine. Jack, Emily and Rosie dragged him away from the edge. Scott lay gasping for a moment, before being engulfed in a group hug by everyone – including Drift.

But it was only a short hug!

They were all far too eager to see what was in the bag. Scott placed it on the ground. It looked just like an ordinary blue sports bag, the kind you'd take your PE kit to school in. 'It could be dangerous,' he warned. 'Stand back! I'll open it from a distance.' He untied the wire hook from the plaited string and attached it to the end of a long stick. Then he hooked it through the little hole in the zip tag, and began to tug *very* slowly.

Emily, Jack and Rosie stood in a circle, all craning their necks to see what was inside.

Eleven

Expect the Unexpected

J ack was so excited he could hardly look. He was sure the bag would contain something mind-blowing: a nuclear missile, a cocoon pulsing with the larvae of an alien life form, the skull of the missing goat …

But what he saw was even more unexpected than all the unexpected things he'd been expecting – three flat, white cardboard boxes.

'Takeaway pizzas!' Emily groaned. 'Is that all?'

Rosie slumped to the ground, her hair over her face. 'I was really hoping this would help us find Gran.'

Scott poked the bag with the stick to make sure it wasn't booby-trapped. Then he lifted the boxes out and stacked them on top of each other.

Jack sat down next to Rosie and reassessed the situation. OK, so takeaway pizza wasn't exactly the clue of the century but, looking on the bright side, it was nearly lunchtime and he *was* a bit peckish. If the pizza hadn't been in the ravine too long it should be perfectly edible!

He flipped up the lid of the top box.

But there was no pizza. The box was stuffed full of newspapers. At least, it looked that way at first, but when he tore a page away, Jack found there was only one layer of newspaper. There was something else underneath.

Money!

Loads of money!

Jack stared in disbelief at bundle upon bundle of crisp pink fifty-pound notes.

Scott opened the other two boxes. They were packed with cash too! Jack had never seen so much money in his life.

Rosie stared at the cash, her eyes round with worry. 'If my gran's been kidnapped, this could be a ransom payment ...'

'But who would have paid it?' Scott asked. 'Your mum hasn't received a ransom demand, has she?'

Rosie shook her head. 'She doesn't have this kind of money anyway.'

While the others examined the cash, Emily seemed more interested in the newspaper. 'Look at this!'

Scott frowned. 'I'm looking but I can't understand any of it.'

'Exactly!' Emily said. 'It's not in English. I'm pretty sure it's Dutch.'

'Dutch?' Rosie asked. 'You mean like ...'

Emily nodded. '... like the key Jack found in the stream.'

'It could be a coincidence,' Scott suggested.

Emily didn't look convinced. She didn't believe in coincidences.

Jack, meanwhile, was investigating the bottom of the bag, just in case there were any *real* forgotten snacks in there. The thought of pizza had made him hungry. He tipped the bag upside down and a shiny metal flask rolled out. Jack sighed with disappointment. It looked like one of those travel mugs for coffee. He didn't even like coffee. He picked it up and gave it a shake.

Whatever was inside, it wasn't coffee! It sounded more like sugar or lentils or ...

Jack twisted off the lid. 'Diamonds!' he breathed.

'Diamonds?' Scott laughed. 'Yeah, right!'

Jack handed him the flask. 'Just don't drop it!'

Scott peeped inside. Jack was telling the truth! The flask was full of tiny sparkling diamonds.

With shaking hands, Scott poured a sprinkle of glittering gems into his palm. They felt cold against his skin and flashed pink and blue and green as they caught the sunlight.

Emily stared at the diamonds for a long moment before turning to Rosie. 'Your gran must have stumbled across a gang of diamond smugglers or major-league bank robbers. She saw too much so they've taken her hostage to keep her quiet.'

Normally Jack and Scott would have rolled their eyes when Emily started on about smugglers and bank robbers, but this time it was hard to argue with the evidence under their noses.

What exactly Dr Armitage had seen and *how* the bag of cash and diamonds had ended up in the ravine remained a mystery. So did the question of *where* the criminals were holding Dr Armitage.

Emily took photos of the evidence while the others counted the money. There were ten bundles of one hundred fifty-pound notes in each of the three boxes: one hundred and fifty thousand pounds in total!

They'd just finished packing everything back into the bag, when Emily noticed that Drift's ears had pricked up into Listening Formation. She signalled for the others to be silent. They could all hear footsteps now. Scott snatched up the bag and they dived for cover behind an outcrop of rock.

Emily peeped out through a crack. At first, looking

straight into the sunlight, the figure she saw walking towards the ravine was no more than a dark silhouette. But gradually Emily made out black boots, a leather jacket and aviator sunglasses, which reflected a flare of dazzling light.

Suddenly she remembered the World War Two pilots. *We've disturbed their ghosts by entering the ravine!* Emily shuddered but, as the figure came closer, she saw it wasn't a ghost but a slimly built man in black leather motorbike trousers and jacket. His face was hidden by a combination of the sunglasses, a mop of shaggy fair hair and a woolly, rambling beard.

Emily felt a movement next to her and noticed that Drift was about to run out and give away their position – just as he had done when they were hiding from Don Penrose. She wondered what had got into her faithful Right Hand Dog lately! She grabbed him by the collar just in time.

The man prowled along the edge of the ravine, his leathers creaking as he walked. He kept his head down, eyes fixed on the ground.

He was searching for something!

You didn't need to be Sherlock Holmes, Emily thought, to figure out that that *something* was a big bag of cash and diamonds – the one that Scott was now hugging to his chest as if it were his favourite teddy.

The man stopped. He kicked at the old parachute sack that was still lying on the ground. He crouched and picked it up, clearly wondering where it had come from. He examined the slide marks where Scott had gone over the edge. Then he shaded his eyes with his hand and swivelled slowly round, scanning the empty moors.

'A bearded man in motorbike gear,' Rosie whispered, peeping out over Emily's shoulder. 'He must be the one who took Gran away.'

Emily nodded. She was looking at the man's boots. He had very small feet; maybe as small as a size six and a half, even ...

'Shhh!' Scott breathed. 'He's coming this way.'

They all held their breath as the man passed the rock. At last he sighed, turned round and began to walk back across the moors.

Rosie and Emily leaped up. 'We've got to follow him!' Rosie said.

'Definitely,' Emily agreed.

Jack gave a thumbs-up. 'What are we waiting for?'

Scott dropped the bag and held up his hands. 'Hang on! We can't *all* follow him. That'd be a parade, not a stake-out!'

'Well, it's *my* gran he's got, so I'm going!' Rosie snapped.

Emily planted her hands on her hips and faced Scott down. 'So am I!' But at that moment she heard a beep on her phone. A text message had arrived. 'It's Mum,' Emily groaned through gritted teeth. 'She wants me to go to the chemist in Tregower and pick up some more medicine for Miss Wendover. Dr Mishra's just been to see her again and says she needs it straight away.'

'That settles it,' Scott said. 'I'll go with Rosie. You and Jack go to the chemist.'

Jack opened his mouth to protest but there was no time. Motorbike Man was already disappearing into the distance. Rosie was pulling Scott's arm.

'We'll call you as soon as we know what's happening,' Scott whispered over his shoulder. 'Don't call the police until you hear from us – it might put Dr Armitage in more danger if they show up at the wrong moment.'

Jack and Emily had no choice but to watch them go. 'Who made Scott the Great Leader all of a sudden?' Jack grumbled. 'Who does he think he is? Genghis Khan?' He stuffed his hands in his pockets and began to stomp back towards the bikes.

Emily called Drift and marched after Jack. 'Attila the Hun, more like!' she fumed, even though she knew it wasn't really Scott's fault she had to go to pick up the medicine.

They'd only taken three steps when Jack and Emily stopped and turned to face each other. 'The bag!' they chorused. 'We've left it behind!'

They ran back to the rocks and Jack hoisted the sports bag onto his shoulder. 'What are we going to do with it?'

'We can't leave it here,' Emily said.

Jack shrugged. 'I could stuff it under my mattress.'

'You can't do that! It'd be stealing!'

'What do you suggest then?' Jack asked.

'We should hide it in a safe place until we know what's going on.'

'What about the hollow tree hideout?' Jack offered. 'The one we used as an HQ in Operation Drowning Man. Nobody goes there – apart from squirrels.'

Drift looked up hopefully. Maybe this time there really *would* be some squirrels to chase!

Emily held up her hand for a high-five. 'Genius idea! You can take it while I go to Tregower.'

—

Jack cycled along the road across the moors. With his backpack on one shoulder and the bag of loot slung over the other, progress was decidedly wobbly.

He couldn't believe he actually had one hundred and fifty thousand pounds in cash about his person! And he was sure the diamonds were worth millions. *Which means*, Jack thought, *that right now I'm technically a millionaire.*

Maybe even a billionaire!

He turned onto the road that headed north towards the causeway and started looking out for the track that would take him to the old hollow willow tree that stood next to a stream near the coast. As he pedalled, Jack daydreamed about spending millions of pounds. He pictured himself walking into a swanky car showroom in Chelsea. 'I'll have two of those Ferraris. Oh, and why not throw in that red Porsche, just for fun? Yes, I'll be paying in cash!'

'You alright, mate?'

Jack jammed on his brakes and snapped his head up at the sound of the voice. It came from one of a group of teenaged boys who were spray-painting graffiti on the side of a bus stop. He'd cycled right into the middle of them.

Jack felt his stomach sink to his trainers.

This would be absolutely the worst ever day in the history of the universe to be mugged!

Twelve

Crime Reconstruction

'Talking to yourself? That's the first sign of madness, you know!' The leader of the gang of graffiti-artists swaggered towards Jack. He was about seventeen, hunched over and skinny. As he spoke he glanced at Jack's Nike bag from under the hood of his sweatshirt.

Jack felt like a bank robber on the run – he might as well have a pair of tights over his head, a black-and-white striped jumper and the word SWAG printed down the side of the bag. He tried to push the bag further behind his back to hide it. Surely the gang could see the money and diamonds glowing through the thin blue nylon as if it were in one of those X-ray scanners at the airport.

'Are you off to the gym?' the gang-leader asked, thrusting his hands into the pockets of his low-slung black jeans.

'Oh, er, yeah, that's right. Off for a workout!' Jack knew he was babbling but he couldn't stop. 'Just me and my good old *ordinary* gym kit.' He patted the bag, his hand hitting one of the pizza boxes, which produced the kind of slapping noise that no ordinary gym kit would make. 'Got my special weights in here,' he said. 'They're very flat, very square.' He pretended to look at his watch even though he wasn't wearing one. 'Well, got to dash! Appointment with my personal trainer.'

With that, Jack pedalled off so fast his bike did a wheelie.

'Have a good one!' the boys called after him, as they went back to their artwork.

By the time he'd safely stowed the bag under piles of dead leaves inside the hollow tree, Jack was in urgent need of a visit to Dotty's Tea Rooms. After all, he *had* single-handedly rescued his brother from certain death in a bottomless ravine *and* fought off a gang of ferocious muggers so far this morning; if that didn't merit a Super Special pizza with extra pineapple and chilli, a double portion of chips and an immense slice of chocolate fudge cake, he didn't know what did!

─

Meanwhile, Emily cycled to Tregower. The tiny chemist shop on the main street of the village was empty and it was only a matter of minutes before Emily was back outside with the medicine for Miss Wendover. As she popped it into the basket on the back of her bike next to Drift, she glanced up at the elegant grey stone house next door. A small brass plaque gleamed in the sunlight on the wall next to the door. Of course! This was Dr Armitage's surgery.

Emily checked the time. Surely it wouldn't hurt to do a quick recce before she went home. It would only take a minute. She could walk up the path and ring at the door, just as Motorbike Man had done in the night. It would be like one of those crime reconstructions they did on TV, with actors playing the parts of the criminals and victims. She'd always wanted to do one of those.

Emily knew that the black door with the plaque was just for patients visiting the doctor's surgery. Instead she wheeled her bike along to the other end of the house, where a gate in the garden wall opened onto a path leading up to a second door. This was the one that the Armitage family used; the one Motorbike Man must have come to in order to find Dr Armitage in the middle of the night.

Emily propped her bike against the wall and walked up the path. She looked up at the windows above the front door. One of them had a sparkly dragon ornament and a row of books on the sill. That had to be Rosie's room!

Emily rang the bell. It was answered by a woman in a quilted dressing gown. She was clutching a hot water bottle and a mug of Lemsip, but she managed a smile.

'Hello, I'm Emily Wild, Rosie's friend,' Emily said.

'That's nice. Sorry I look such a state. I've got flu.' Rosie's mum raised her eyebrows, obviously waiting to find out why Emily was calling.

Emily rooted in her bag and pulled out a pack of scented soaps. She'd been carrying it around for months; according to *Survival Guide for Secret Agents*, a small multi-purpose gift that could be handed over in a variety of undercover situations was a vital component of a good secret agent's toolkit. 'I heard you were ill so I brought you these,' she said.

Rosie's mum took the soaps and smelled them. 'Er, that's kind of you, thanks.' She still looked puzzled.

'Oh, yeah,' Emily said quickly. 'The reason I'm here is just to say don't worry if Rosie's not back for a while. She's out with some friends, er, going for a hike on the moors!' *Well, that's true*, Emily thought, *last time I saw Rosie she was hiking after Motorbike Man with Scott!*

'It's good that she's out in the fresh air instead of inside with her nose in a book all day,' Rosie's mum said as she began to close the door.

Emily stood on the doorstep feeling most dejected. She hadn't had a chance to ask half the questions she'd planned. Her feeble attempt at a crime reconstruction had been a waste of time! And, meanwhile, Scott and Rosie were getting all the action, tracking their prime suspect without her! Slowly she began to trudge back down the path.

Something tugged at her back. She whipped round to find that a straggling branch from a rose bush had caught the hem of her t-shirt. As she looked down to unsnag the thorn she glimpsed something shiny out of the corner of her eye. A small silver stud button was lying on top of the low lavender hedge that bordered the path. She picked it up. It was just a button. It probably belonged to Rosie or her mum or her gran.

Or, Emily wondered, as she slipped it into an evidence pouch and popped it into her bag, *could it have fallen off a black leather motorbike jacket?*

—

Jack threw open the door of Dotty's Tea Rooms and lurched towards the counter. '*Emergency!*' he gasped, clutching his stomach, 'I need pizza and I need it fast!' He looked up, laughing, expecting to see Dotty smiling back at him, but instead it was Mrs White from Roshendra Farm.

Seeing Jack's surprise, she smiled as she smoothed her white apron over her plump middle. 'No Dotty today, I'm afraid.'

Jack stared at her. He couldn't remember Dotty ever leaving her post at the café before. It would take something serious to keep her away. He gulped. First the goat, then Dr Armitage, now Dotty! All these disappearances! Perhaps a band of aliens really was abducting Earthlings! *Why didn't they take me when they had the chance?* he wondered. He was starting to take it personally!

Mrs White wiped a cloth over the counter. 'Dotty called me this morning and said she was too sick to open the café today. I'm standing in for her.' She shook her head. 'That girl's been working much too hard. She's been looking very tired lately.'

Jack thought for a moment. It was true. Dotty had looked a bit rough when they'd called in for breakfast the other day. He'd thought she was just worried about those phantom lights dragging people into swamps, but maybe she'd been coming down with something. 'Could be this flu that's going round,' he said.

Mrs White nodded. 'Now, what can I get you?'

Jack gave his order.

Mrs White laughed. 'You *are* hungry!'

'It's been a busy morning!'

Jack took his Coke, sat down at a table in the corner and scanned the cartoon page of an old Sunday paper while he waited for his food. He wondered whether Scott and Rosie had found out what Motorbike Man was up to yet. Knowing Scott, he'd be showing off to Rosie and playing the big hero. It was so unfair! If Scott solved the Mystery of the Disappearing Gran or the Mystery of the Dodgy Lights all by himself, Jack would never talk to him again!

In fact, Jack was so busy thinking about Motorbike Man he could swear he heard a motorbike roaring along the seafront and purring to a stop outside. The bell on the café door jangled. Jack looked up.

He really *had* heard a motorbike!

The man who'd just entered Dotty's Tea Rooms was wearing black motorbike leathers and carrying a red and silver helmet.

He also had a bushy blond beard.

And, Jack realized, as the man pulled a stool up to the counter and began to talk to Mrs White, *he looks familiar!*

Jack tried to think where he'd seen him before. It wasn't the man they'd spied at the ravine. This guy was much bigger.

Then he remembered! This was the man who'd been sitting outside the café at the next table the morning after the glow-worm camp. *The man I accidentally hit with a sugar cube!*

Suddenly Jack's heart was galloping. *We were talking about the phantom lights that morning. He could easily have overheard us.*

Were Scott and Rosie stalking the wrong bearded biker across the moors?

Was the real suspect right here ordering a double espresso?

Someone had to find out.

And Jack Carter was the man for the job!

Thirteen

A Secret Meeting

The slim, bearded man in the motorbike gear headed up the slope from the ravine towards the top of the ridge. As he hurried along, he kept stopping and glancing around. This made the job of following him extremely difficult. Every time he looked back, Scott and Rosie had to throw themselves into a clump of bracken or a gorse bush. Before long they were covered in bruises and studded with thorns.

At last, near the top of the ridge, the man stopped and patted his leather jacket as if looking for something. From their hiding position in a shallow gully, Scott heard the sound of a phone ringtone. To his surprise it was Beyoncé's *All the Single Ladies*. Motorbike Man took his phone from his pocket and answered with a gruff, 'Yes?'

Scott frowned at Rosie. The man's voice was so quiet they could barely hear him. *Probably muffled by that overgrown hairball of a beard*, Scott thought. *It must be like having a small sheepdog strapped to your chin.* He vowed at that moment he would *never* grow a beard. He'd seen far too many bad ones lately. He tugged Rosie's arm and they commando-crawled as close as they dared.

Motorbike Man did a lot of listening to someone at the other end of the line. Then he nodded and scratched at his beard. 'Yes! I've got it. Bamton Towers.' He spoke in a London accent – although it sounded a bit phoney to Scott's ears, like an American actor doing a London accent in a movie. 'Yeah, I'll deliver, mate,' Motorbike Man went on. 'Don't you worry!' Then he hung up and continued on his way. Within a few minutes he'd disappeared down the other side of the ridge.

Scott and Rosie scrambled up after him, but when they reached the top Motorbike Man was nowhere to be seen. 'Oh, no, we've lost him!' Rosie groaned.

But Scott had glimpsed a movement near a small flat-roofed hut a little way down the hill. 'Down there,' he said, pointing.

Scott and Rosie picked their way along a goat path down the hill. As they drew closer to the small building, Scott could see from its hexagonal shape and the tiny square windows set into the concrete walls that it was a World War Two pillbox. He knew from his history lessons that they'd been built all round the coast of Britain in case the Germans tried to invade. Those windows were gun ports for the men inside to shoot through. This was one of the highest points on the island, with a perfect view across the moors and dunes towards Westward Beach, where German boats could have landed.

But the only Germans who came to Castle Key island these days were tourists, so what was Motorbike Man up to in the old pillbox?

He must be having a secret meeting with his criminal contacts, Scott thought. *We need to tread very carefully. If that hut's full of bank robbers or diamond smugglers, they're not exactly going to welcome uninvited visitors in for tea and biscuits.*

Motioning for Rosie to keep silent, Scott tiptoed towards the pillbox. There were rocks scattered around the outside and, by climbing up onto them, he was just tall enough to see in through one of the gun ports. It took a few moments for his eyes to adapt to the gloom of the interior after the bright sunlight, but gradually he made out three people inside the pillbox, which was little more than an empty concrete shell.

Motorbike Man was pacing round in circles talking to another much bigger man who was lying propped up against a wall smoking a cigarette. This guy didn't have a beard, although thick stubble suggested he'd not shaved for some time. He was wearing a white basketball vest, which showed off body-builder arms. His skin was dark and shiny with sweat. His jeans had been cut open along the side seam and his leg was bound with bandages and a splint. The third person – who was kneeling down checking the injured leg – was a woman. A woman with short white hair, wearing tweedy trousers, a blue shirt with the sleeves rolled up and beige suede desert boots.

Scott clambered down from the rocks and turned to Rosie, who was bouncing up and down on her toes, bursting with impatience.

'Is Gran in there?' she whispered.

Scott nodded. 'Don't worry. She looks fine.' He knelt down and laced his fingers together to give Rosie a leg-up. 'Have a look for yourself.'

After a moment, Rosie jumped down. 'That's Gran alright,' she whispered, with a huge smile. 'She must have been so busy helping this guy that she lost track of time.' Rosie turned and began running over the rocks to the other side of the pillbox.

Scott scrambled after her. 'Don't do anything until we know what's going on ...'

But it was too late. Before he could get the words *It might be dangerous* out of his mouth, Rosie was already barrelling in through the door.

'Hi, Gran! There you are!' she cried.

Scott sank back against the wall, his heart in freefall. He swallowed hard and peeped in round the frame of the open door.

Rosie was standing with her back to him in the middle of the pillbox. A shaft of light from one of the gun ports was shining down on her, illuminating the top of her hair like a halo. Motorbike Man, Dr Armitage and the injured guy were all staring at her with their mouths wide open.

Rosie took a step forwards, holding out her arms for a hug. 'I've been so worried about you, Gran ...' But her words died away. The man with the bad leg was reaching for something at his side.

'Rosie, get out!' Dr Armitage screamed. 'Run!'

But it was too late.

The man with the bad leg had a gun.

And he was pointing it straight at Rosie.

Fourteen

Into the Line of Fire

Scott could hardly believe his eyes. He shrank back against the wall, shaking from head to foot. He was meant to be keeping Rosie safe and he'd let her walk straight into the line of fire! He squinted round the door again. The injured man was poking the gun – a serious-looking double-barrelled sawn-off shotgun – at Rosie.

'Is there anyone else with you?' he barked. His accent sounded European, maybe Swedish or Dutch ...

'No, I'm on my own,' Rosie replied in a small but steady voice.

Now Scott felt even worse. Rosie hadn't given him away.

'You'd better be!' the injured man growled, blowing out a last puff of smoke and stubbing his cigarette out on the dusty concrete floor.

'Leave my granddaughter alone!' Dr Armitage snapped. 'You great bully!'

The man turned his gun on her and sneered. 'Nobody asked you!'

'You should show a bit more respect, young man,' Dr Armitage told him. 'I don't *have* to treat this broken leg, you know!'

But the guy just grinned and waved the gun. 'That's what you think!'

Scott's gut instincts were screaming at him to rush in, overpower the injured man and rescue Rosie and her gran. But his brain pointed out that Motorbike Man was probably carrying a gun as well – in which case, he'd almost certainly end up being captured and held hostage too. That was the kind of thing Jack would do! Scott knew that the best hope of rescue was to sneak away before he was discovered and find help. That was the smart option, and he was about to take it when the man with the broken leg started talking to Motorbike Man. Scott hesitated. Maybe he could pick up some useful information about what they were up to.

'Right, Steve,' the injured man said. 'You're sure it's all sorted then?'

Motorbike Man – or Steve, as it seemed he was called – nodded. 'Yeah. Like I told you, mate. The boss said I'm to take you to—'

His next words were drowned out by a furious roar from the man with the broken leg. 'Shut it, you herbert! Don't say where we're going. We can't have these two knowing!' He slapped his forehead, then winced as the movement jolted his bad leg. 'I hate working with *amateurs*!'

'Yeah, right, sorry,' the bearded man mumbled. He was still pacing the room. Scott could almost see the stress coming off him in waves. 'So, anyway, I'm to take you to *you know where*. I've hired a car and driven it up the track as close as I can. We'll have to carry you to it.'

The man with the broken leg nodded. 'Let's do it.'

Motorbike Steve leaned against the wall as if trying to look casual. He wasn't succeeding. 'Then we're letting these two go, right? We won't need them any more.'

'No way! They're my insurance policy. Just in case you get any dumb ideas about double-crossing us.' The injured man shot Steve a suspicious look. He took another cigarette from a pack on the floor and lit it. 'I'm still not convinced you haven't kept that last delivery that got "lost on the moors" for yourself.'

A delivery lost on the moors? Scott wondered. Surely the man had to be talking about the bag of diamonds and money in the ravine! But he didn't have time to give it any more thought. The injured man was still talking.

'How do I know you're not planning to do a runner and call the police to pick the rest of us up?'

Steve snorted with laughter, his beard bobbing up and down. 'I wouldn't do that, mate. Honest! But if we take these two with us, they'll know where the boss's place is, won't they? You said yourself, we can't have that.'

The man with the broken leg grinned and tapped his nose. 'We blindfold them!'

Steve gave a thumbs-up. 'Good thinking. *Then* we let them go?'

'Yeah, yeah. As soon as we're sure you've kept your word, one of our men will drive them to somewhere in the middle of nowhere and let them go. But if I so much as *see* a policeman, they're for it. And so are you! Know what I mean?' Just in case Steve *didn't* know what he meant, the injured man mimed shooting Steve in the chest. Since he was holding a sawn-off shotgun in his hand, the mime was disturbingly realistic.

Steve shrugged. 'Fair enough.'

'Now, tie that one's hands behind her back so she doesn't try any funny business.' The man with the bad leg jabbed the gun in Rosie's direction. 'Then you,' he pointed at Dr Armitage, who was glaring at him as if she'd like to give his leg a swift kick, 'help Steve lift me to the car.'

That, Scott thought, *is definitely my cue to get out of here.*

He scrambled over the rocks and sprinted back up the goat path as fast his legs would go. As soon as he was over the brow of the ridge he ducked down so that he still had a view of the pillbox. He pulled his phone from his pocket. His hands were shaking so much he could hardly open his contact list and select the name.

—

Emily was almost home when her phone rang. She stood down from the pedals and took her phone from her bag. To her relief she saw Scott's name on the display. She'd been wondering why it was taking him so long to call with an update.

'Emily! That you?'

Emily could hardly make out her name. Scott was panting as if he'd just completed the London Marathon. 'What's up?' she asked. 'Are you OK? What about Rosie?'

At last Scott managed to gasp out the story. 'They've been holding … Dr Armitage … at the old pillbox. They've got Rosie now too. But they're about to move to another location. I heard Motorbike Man say the name of the place they're going on the phone. Bamton Towers. Do you know where that is?'

Emily watched a fleet of fishing boats chugging across the harbour. She'd never heard of Bamton Towers. This was a disaster! Now Rosie had been captured as well as her gran, and they had no idea where the men were taking them. *We should never have let Rosie get involved in the investigation in the first place. I should have known it was too dangerous for an amateur.* 'Are you sure he said *Bamton* Towers?' she demanded.

'I think that was it,' Scott said. 'But we weren't very close and he really mumbles with that great big beard.'

'*Bamton, bamton* ...' Emily repeated, racking her brains. Suddenly, it came to her. 'Oh, I know, could it have been *Barrington* Towers?'

'Yes!' Scott said. 'That's it! So where is Barrington Towers?'

'It's this enormous posh house on the seafront in Carrickstowe. It's owned by some billionaire businessman called Peter Barrington. His company makes parts for mobile phones.'

'Yes, I'm sure that's the place,' Scott said excitedly. 'They mentioned *the boss*. That must be this Peter Barrington guy.'

'Right!' Emily said. 'I'll call Detective Inspector Hassan. The police could be there in minutes.'

'No!' Scott spluttered. 'We can't do that. The injured guy said if he even *saw* a policeman Rosie and her gran would be for it. We can't risk putting them in danger.'

Emily thought for a moment. 'OK. We'll go to

Barrington Towers ourselves and make sure they let Rosie and Dr Armitage go.'

'What? On our bikes?' Scott snorted. 'They've got a car. We'll never get there in time.'

Emily watched a seagull plunge headfirst into the waves and reappear with a fish flapping in its beak. Scott could be so negative sometimes! 'There are roadworks on the causeway,' she pointed out. 'That'll slow them down. And you said they'd got to carry the guy with the broken leg to the car first.'

There was a pause on the end of the line. 'Yeah, that's true,' Scott said. 'They haven't even left the pillbox yet. OK, it's worth a try.'

Emily looked at her watch. It was two thirty. 'Meet you at the pier on Carrickstowe seafront at fifteen hundred hours. Barrington Towers is just a couple of minutes from there—'

'I can see them coming out now,' Scott interrupted.

'We'd better get a move on then.'

Scott was already running down the hill. 'I'll call Jack on my way,' he panted.

Emily jumped back onto the pedals, raced along the promontory path at breakneck speed, threw down her bike so fast that Drift only just hopped out of the basket in time, and flung open the door of The Lighthouse. Her mum was in the guest lounge tidying the magazines on the coffee table. Emily thrust Miss Wendover's medicine into her arms and bolted back out of the door before it had even swung shut. 'Can't stop! Bye!' she called over her shoulder. She grabbed her bike and flipped it round. As Drift jumped into the basket she checked the time. She had twenty-seven minutes and ten seconds to get to Carrickstowe.

She could do it.

Just!

Fifteen

Jack on the Case Again

Not far away, in Dotty's Tea Rooms, Jack was eavesdropping on his new suspect, aka the Viking Biker. It wasn't just the bushy blond beard that had prompted Jack to give the man this name: he was as tall and broad as a grizzly bear. All he needed to complete the Viking image was a pair of elk horns sticking out of the motorbike helmet that he held under his arm as he leaned against the cake counter talking to Mrs White.

Jack held the newspaper in front of his face and pretended to be engrossed in the Garfield cartoon. He was, of course, peeping over the top of the page. He was quite sure this was the man Rosie had seen drive off with her gran in the night.

'Have you seen Dotty?' the Viking Biker was asking Mrs White.

'She's off sick, dear,' Mrs White told him.

The Viking Biker sank down onto a barstool. 'That's strange. I just called at her flat. She's not there.'

Jack could hardly believe his ears. The Viking Biker had a foreign accent! Jack couldn't be sure, but he'd be willing to bet at least half the contents of the pizza box in the hollow tree that it was a *Dutch* accent. And they had two Dutch clues already – the key from the stream and the newspaper packed in with the money and diamonds! It was all falling into place. The Viking Biker must be their diamond smuggler!

Jack's hands were trembling with such excitement he could hardly hold the newspaper. Garfield was jumping up and down in front of his eyes as he tuned back into the conversation at the counter.

'Dotty was probably just asleep,' Mrs White suggested. 'There's a nasty flu bug going round.' She hurried to the pizza oven and looked inside. 'Almost ready!' she called to Jack. Jack lowered the paper for a moment and gave a thumbs-up.

The Viking Biker shook his head. 'I checked inside Dotty's flat. I've got a key. No sign of her.'

Mrs White raised her eyebrows in surprise.

The Viking Biker laughed. 'Oh, sorry, I should have said. I'm Sven, Dotty's boyfriend.' He reached across the counter to shake Mrs White's hand.

'Oh, yes,' Mrs White said, smiling as she topped up his coffee cup. 'Dotty's talked about you. You're a pastry chef in Truro, aren't you?'

Jack almost dropped the paper. *A pastry chef? Yeah, right! So that's your cover story, is it?* No doubt poor Dotty had no idea that her so-called boyfriend was really a granny-stealing diamond-dealer. He'd been telling her a pack of lies! Jack disguised his snort of anger as a sneeze.

Then he had a truly terrible thought. *What if Sven was lying about not being able to find Dotty?*

What if he'd *killed* her?

'Bless you!' Mrs White called to Jack.

'I wasn't going to come over to Castle Key until the weekend,' the Viking Biker went on, 'but Dotty hasn't been answering her phone since I last saw her on Friday morning. I'm getting worried.' He sighed. 'Maybe she's gone to see the doctor. I'll go back to her flat and try again.' He got up from the stool. 'Thanks for the coffee.' And with that, he made for the door.

Behind the paper, Jack was in a dilemma. He knew he should follow the Viking Biker to see what he was up to.

He could hear Emily's voice in his ear telling him that a proper investigator would *never* let a suspect slip the net – especially not a *murder* suspect! But, on the other hand, Mrs White had just this second taken his pizza out of the oven. It smelled like heaven on a plate! His stomach was advising him – very strongly – to ignore Emily, stay put and eat his pizza.

His stomach could be very persuasive!

Yes, quite right, Jack thought, *I'll stay here*.

But Emily – even *imaginary* Emily – didn't like to be ignored. '*He's getting away!*' she yelled.

Suddenly Jack had a brainwave. If he could waylay the Viking Biker before he left the café, he could keep his suspect in sight *and* eat his pizza! He could probably extract some useful information from him into the bargain. That would keep Emily off his back. He might even retrieve his notebook from where he'd thrown it in the tree house the other day so he could write up this interview later. *Oh, yeah*, he thought. *Jack Carter is on the case again!* He dropped the paper and called to Sven, who was reaching for the door handle. 'Excuse me! I couldn't help hearing. You're looking for Dotty?'

Sven walked towards Jack's table, where he flipped a chair round and sat down with his arms folded on the back. 'Yes, that's right. Do you know where she is?'

Jack gulped. What with the rumpus between virtual Emily and his stomach he hadn't really thought through the next step of this brainwave. Then he remembered, he *did* have an idea. 'I think she's been abducted by aliens,' he said.

'Aliens?' Sven repeated.

'Yeah, there's been a spate of alien abductions going on round here lately.'

Sven gaped at Jack with a blank expression. 'Aliens?'

For a master criminal, Jack thought, *this guy's a bit dim!* 'Yeah, first it was a goat,' he explained slowly. 'Then a doctor. Now Dotty's disappeared. Actually, I saw the UFO landing on the first night … but I managed to get away.'

Sven opened his mouth, but before he could stammer 'Aliens?' for the third time, two things happened at once.

Mrs White placed Jack's Super Special pizza with extra pineapple and chilli on the table.

And Jack's phone rang.

Jack glanced at the display. It was Scott. 'Hang on a sec,' Jack told Sven. He listened as Scott panted out his instructions. Then he hung up and pushed back his chair. 'Sorry, I've got to go!'

'That'd be the *aliens* calling, would it?' Sven muttered.

Jack looked at Sven as if he'd gone mad. 'Of course not! It was my brother. He needs me for an urgent rescue mission in Carrickstowe.'

Sven shook his head. 'Silly me,' he said sarcastically. 'Of course he does!'

Jack took a last longing look at the pizza and made for the door.

He was halfway out when he felt a tap on his shoulder.

Mrs White handed him a pizza box. 'Why don't you take it with you?'

—

Scott arrived on Carrickstowe seafront first. He was cooling down in the shade of an ice-cream van at the entrance to the pier when Emily and Jack screeched to a halt behind him. Emily glanced at her watch as she jumped off her bike. 'Twenty-six minutes. That's a new record!'

'Guess what?' Jack puffed. 'I found the man who kidnapped Dr Armitage. He's pretending to be Dotty's boyfriend. But he's *Dutch*!' He grinned and mimicked the Viking Biker's accent. 'Hello, I'm Sven the pastry chef from Truro!' The grin fell from his face as he remembered the other thing he'd found out. 'I think he's murdered Dotty as well.'

Emily stared at Jack for a long moment. Then she blinked. 'Dotty's boyfriend *is* called Sven. He's not Dutch, he's Swedish. And he *is* a pastry chef from Truro. Dotty's told me about him loads of times. He's won awards for his chocolate éclairs.'

Jack was speechless.

'Anyway,' Scott said. 'Getting back to reality. We *know* who kidnapped Dr Armitage. The Motorbike Man we saw on the moors. And he's still got her. And

Rosie too. They're on their way to Barrington Towers.' He turned to Emily. 'Where is this place? We've got to get there fast! They're on their way in Motorbike Man's hire car.'

Emily got back on her bike. 'This way!'

The three friends raced along the seafront past the funfair, the trampolines and the bandstand. Just before they came to the marina, where boats of every shape and size were moored, Emily stopped and pointed to a two-metre-high white wall set back from the road. The row of security cameras and the black electric gates between colossal brick gateposts topped with gold lions all suggested that the house hidden behind the wall was no ordinary semi-detached.

It was like a fortress.

A very upmarket fortress!

'That,' Emily whispered as they propped their bikes against a fence on the other side of the road, 'is Barrington Towers.'

Drift jumped down from his basket and they all took up position behind a parked van. While they watched for the hire car to come along the road, Scott filled Emily and Jack in on the details of what he'd seen at the pillbox. 'As well as Motorbike Man, there's another guy. It looks like he's broken his leg. They mean business! They've got guns.'

'But Dr Armitage and Rosie are both OK?' Jack asked.

Scott nodded. 'I think they just kidnapped Dr Armitage to help with the broken leg. The accident must have happened out on the moor that night. They're bringing the injured man here to get help. He said they'll drive Dr Armitage and Rosie somewhere and release them as soon as he and 'the boss' are sure Motorbike Man hasn't double-crossed them and called the police.'

Jack looked up and down the road. It was deserted apart from two small boys walking towards the pier with fishing nets over their shoulders. 'No police anywhere. So there should be no problem.'

'Well, we're here to make sure of that,' Emily said with a determined jut of her chin.

At that moment they heard a car driving up the road.

A silver Ford Mondeo slowed and rolled to a stop outside the gates of Barrington Towers.

Sixteen

The Pizza Plan

'This is it,' Emily breathed, lowering her binoculars from her eyes. 'It's a hire car. I can see the logo on the windscreen.' She looked again. 'And, yes, that's Motorbike Man driving.'

The black gates swished open as smoothly as velvet curtains.

The car slipped through.

The gates slid shut.

'What do we do now?' Jack asked.

'Wait for them to come back out,' Scott said.

'Then what?'

'We follow,' Emily said. 'Let's hope they don't go too far.'

Crouched behind the van, they waited for the gates to open. The sun beat down, its heat doubling as it bounced off the van and the pavement. The smell of melting tarmac, hot metal and scorched sand from the beach filled Jack's nostrils. The baleful wailing of gulls and the knocking of ropes on the masts in the marina filled his ears.

Still they waited. The gates didn't open. The car didn't reappear.

Jack thought about the pizza in his backpack.

He knew Scott and Emily would go berserk if he suggested getting it out for a snack. He wondered which would finish him off first: heat stroke or starvation.

Emily sighed and looked at her watch. 'We've been here an hour.'

Thirty minutes later Scott closed his eyes and raked his hair back. 'They're not coming out, are they?'

'I can't believe it!' Jack seethed. 'The liar! After Dr Armitage fixed his leg up too. He promised he'd let them go!'

'People break their promises,' Emily said. 'This is a criminal gang, not the Scouts!'

'We'll have to rescue them,' Scott said in a grim voice. 'We can't risk involving the police.'

They all knew he was right. They stared over the bonnet of the van at the high white wall, the shiny black gates and the security cameras.

'But how are we going to get in?' Scott groaned.

Jack watched a couple walk past sharing a burger and chips from a takeaway box. His stomach growled. It gave him an idea. 'Pizza!' he said.

'How can you think of eating when we're in the middle of a mission?' Emily asked.

'I didn't mean I want to *eat* pizza,' Jack said. 'Well, I do, but that's not the point. I meant, I could ring at the gate and say I'm a delivery boy.' He opened his backpack and pulled out the takeaway pizza Mrs White had given him as he left Dotty's. 'One Super Special to go!'

'Jack, that's genius!' Emily said. 'They'll open the gate for the pizza. And we'll sneak in behind you.' She took a clipboard and pen from her bag. 'Take these. They'll make you look more official. Oh, and this,' she added, handing him a piece of chewing gum. 'Pizza delivery boys always chew gum.'

Scott frowned. It seemed like a very risky plan, but they didn't have any better ones. 'OK. We'll do it. Just one thing. *I'll* be the pizza delivery boy. I'm older. It'll be more believable.'

Before Jack had time to object, Scott had grabbed the

pizza box, the clipboard and the gum and was marching across the road.

—

Scott took a deep breath and pressed the button on the intercom. Who knew what he'd find behind the black gates? But he was responsible for letting Rosie get herself taken hostage in the first place. He had to get her – and her gran – out of here safely.

'Yeah? Who's there?'

'Pizza delivery!' Scott said into the intercom, holding the pizza box up and waving it under the security camera.

'We didn't order pizza,' came the gruff reply.

'This is Barrington Towers, isn't it?'

'Yes!'

'Well, *someone* at this address ordered pizza,' Scott said.

'OK. Bring it in.'

There was a buzz and the gates began to slide back, disappearing into the walls as if by magic.

Scott stood with his mouth open. He'd known the house was going to be impressive, but this was something else!

It was like a film star's Hollywood mansion: all dazzling white walls, smoked-glass windows, walkways and balconies with pillars and arches. There were tall palm trees everywhere, their fronds fluttering in the breeze. He caught a whiff of chlorine in the air and heard sounds of splashing over the bass beat of music from an outdoor speaker. There was definitely a swimming pool somewhere. It was like stepping into a luxury holiday resort ...

'Psst! What's going on?'

Scott snapped back to reality and turned to see Jack, Emily and Drift crouching on the pavement behind him. He held up the pizza box to block the view from the CCTV camera on the gatepost, and gestured for the others to duck down and crawl though the gate. Within seconds they were through and had taken cover behind a bush covered in bright pink flowers.

Scott started walking up the perfectly raked gravel drive towards the front door. On either side, sprinklers sprayed water over sweeping lawns. He walked slowly. He knew he would have only moments to get inside the house before someone took the pizza from him and shut the door in his face. He needed a plan.

Scott climbed the gleaming marble steps with all the speed of a geriatric snail.

He stood between the fluted marble columns.

He chewed gum and took his time pretending to examine an order on the clipboard in case anyone was watching. He still hadn't thought of a plan, but he couldn't delay any longer. He forced himself to reach for the oversized gold knocker in the shape of a lion's head. But, before he could grasp it, the door was opened by a bulky man with a thick neck and bald head, both tattooed with a pattern of flames.

'Whassup?'

Scott held out the box. 'Er, your pizza, sir.'

Flame Head snatched the box from Scott. 'Dotty's Pizzas?' he growled, reading the logo on the top of the box. 'We don't usually get this brand.'

Scott shrugged and chewed his gum. 'That's six pounds, please.'

Flame Head flipped up the lid, folded a slice and bit into it. He nodded as he munched. 'Not bad. I'll take it!' With that he kicked the door shut.

Scott was left staring at the lion's-head door knocker.

The man hadn't paid for the pizza!

But under the circumstances he didn't think it wise to knock again to ask for his money.

And anyway, he'd just noticed something.

Scott nudged the door with his toe. It moved.

It hadn't closed properly.

An open door was worth a million times more than the price of a pizza – even one of Dotty's Super Specials with extra pineapple and chilli!

~

Meanwhile, Jack, Emily and Drift watched from the cover of the pink-flowered bush.

'He's in!' Emily breathed, as they saw Scott slip in through the door.

'Don't forget that was *my* idea,' Jack grumbled. 'What are we meant to do now? Sit here and wait?'

Jack looked at Emily. Emily looked at Jack.

Neither of them were the sitting-and-waiting kind.

'There must be another way in,' Emily said.

'All houses have a back door,' Jack agreed.

Jack looked to the right. *Private swimming pool complete with sun loungers and floating cocktail bar.* He looked to the left. *Enormous garage stuffed with mega-cool sports cars.* This place was awesome – just like one of those gangsta pads in Miami he'd seen on TV! He could hear people at the pool but the garage looked empty. That would be the best bet. All they had to do was cross the miles of wide open lawn to get there. Jack pointed at a fountain halfway across the manicured grass. Emily nodded.

By the time they'd scurried across the lawn and dived behind the fountain – a gold-plated goddess with water spouting from her head into a large pool – they were soaked by the spray of the sprinklers. But at least there were no alarms or sirens.

So far, so good.

Drift shook the water from his coat. He hoped they were going to play the sprinkler game again!

Jack peeped over the low wall that surrounded the fountain pool. He jumped as a fat orange koi carp lunged up through the surface of the water and snapped at a fly. The coast looked clear as far as the garage. Jack beckoned to Emily and they got ready to make a break for it.

That's when they saw the dogs.

Or, rather, that's when they *heard* them.

First came the baying and the howling and the growling.

Then came the three enormous Rottweilers pounding across the lawn.

Seventeen

Double Trouble

*G*uard dogs!

Enormous snarling guard dogs with slavering jaws wide open to reveal flashes of razor-sharp teeth.

Emily was furious with herself as she shrank back behind the fountain. She should have known a house as ritzy as Barrington Towers would be protected by dogs – especially a house that was owned by a man posing as a law-abiding businessman when he was actually running some kind of illegal diamond-smuggling ring!

She glanced back across the lawn. Even if they could outrun the dogs, the gates were firmly shut. There was no escape that way. Struggling to keep her panic at bay, Emily bent down to scoop Drift out of the path of the oncoming hounds.

But Drift had gone. Frantically, Emily looked round for him. To her horror, he was trotting across the lawn, wagging his tail as if the Rottweilers were his long-lost brothers. Then he flipped over and rolled onto his back with his legs in the air.

'What's Drift doing?' Jack gasped. 'Playing dead? He will be if he doesn't get out of their way!'

Emily started to run to help Drift but she stopped, laughing with relief. Drift's rolling-around routine was telling the Rottweilers that he wanted to be friends and was happy for them to be in charge. And it seemed they were getting the message! One of the big black and tan dogs batted him with a paw and backed away. Drift jumped up and batted him back. The other two joined in. All four tails were wagging now!

'They're playing!' Jack laughed.

Emily dug in her bag for the pack of treats she kept for Drift.

The Rottweilers heard the pack rustle. They padded over and sat in a row, looking up at Emily. With their intelligent amber eyes, broad faces and pink tongues hanging from wide, smiley mouths, they looked like three giant teddy bears. Emily gave them each a treat – and one to Drift, of course. The Rottweilers wolfed them down and nudged her hand for second helpings. Emily laughed and gave them all another.

But suddenly Jack saw something. 'Uh-oh!' he breathed. 'We're in for it now.'

Emily looked up to see two beefy men running down the steps of the house onto the lawn.

'They've heard the dogs,' Jack groaned. 'They're coming this way. They're bound to see us in a minute.'

'Not if we set up a distraction,' Emily said. She crouched down and whispered one word in Drift's ear.

Drift panted happily. Runaway was one of his favourite commands! He was more than happy to hare off across the lawn at full speed.

The three Rottweilers shot off after him.

Drift raced towards the pool. The Rottweilers chased him. Drift ran round and round the decking. The Rottweilers chased him some more. Then they began to chase each other.

There were shrieks and squawks as the dogs leaped over the bikini-clad ladies on the loungers. The two henchmen stopped in the middle of the lawn, turned and began jogging back towards the pool, yelling dire threats at the rampaging dogs as they went.

'Will Drift be OK?' Jack asked.

Emily grinned at the sound of an almighty splash.

'He's having a lovely time. He'll come and find us when he's ready.' She tugged at Jack's sleeve. 'Now, let's find a back way into the house while those men are busy dealing with the canine pool party!'

—

Meanwhile, Scott had been wandering around the mansion for what seemed like days. He'd sneaked across a hall the size of a tennis court, decorated with thick white rugs, white leather sofas and enormous black-and-white photos of skyscrapers. He'd crept up a sweeping staircase and prowled the corridors, peeping into lavish bedrooms, walk-in dressing rooms and bathrooms kitted out with saunas and jacuzzis. How was he ever going to find Rosie and her gran? This place was like Buckingham Palace!

At last he came to a huge games room with a jukebox, a pool table and a long cocktail bar made of shiny black marble. One wall was covered with a display of electric guitars. Scott was tempted to go in for a closer look at the guitars, but then he glimpsed a small bearded guy in black leathers sitting in the back corner. It was Motorbike Man! He was slumped over a table with his head in his hands looking dead worried.

Maybe he's in trouble with the boss for some reason, Scott thought. Then he had an idea. *Perhaps he'll help me find Dr Armitage and Rosie. He seemed quite* concerned about them in the pillbox, after all. Scott took a step into the room, but then he hesitated. *How do I know I can trust him? He'll probably just hand me over to the boss.*

Scott had just decided it was a stupid idea and was tiptoeing back out of the door when Motorbike Man glanced up. Scott made it out of the games room just in time to avoid being spotted. But at that moment he heard footsteps approaching and a man talking into a walkie-talkie. 'An intruder? I'll check it out.'

Scott's heart did a backflip. He needed to hide! Without stopping to think about what might be on the other side, he opened the next door along the corridor and slipped through.

He stood for a moment blinking in the dark.

The room smelled of beer and popcorn and he could hear the roar of a crowd.

As Scott's eyes adjusted he saw that he'd walked into a home cinema. Several men were sprawled in plush armchairs watching a football match on a massive screen. Scott did a double take. *It was Chelsea versus Ajax in the Champions League!* He'd been longing to watch this match, but Aunt Kate didn't have any of the sports channels. It looked like Chelsea were one-nil up!

No wonder nobody's noticed me sneaking in at the back, Scott thought, as he ducked down behind a chair and peeped out at the screen – just in time to see Ajax equalize from a penalty.

Scott almost groaned out loud. But, to his amazement, the other viewers all started leaping out of their seats, punching the air and cheering. Why were they all supporting Ajax – a Dutch team from Amsterdam – instead of the English team, Chelsea?

But then Scott remembered. *Of course, this gang has a Dutch connection.* So far, there'd only been small clues: the Dutch newspaper in the pizza box and the key Jack had found on the moors. But this was rock-solid proof! The diamond-smugglers were from Amsterdam and Ajax was their home team.

Scott wished he could stay to watch the rest of the match but he knew he had to continue his search. He was about to slip back out of the door when Chelsea scored another goal. He clapped his hand over his mouth to stifle a cheer. Being caught sneaking around Barrington Towers would be bad enough; giving himself away as a Chelsea supporter in a room full of angry Ajax fans would spell double trouble!

A man with small close-set eyes and long dreadlocks got up from his chair, holding up his mobile phone. 'Back in a minute,' he called to the others. 'The boss has summoned me.'

One of the others threw him a can of beer. 'Hey, Larry, take this to Hank on your way back. He's stuck guarding that doctor and her kid so he's missing the match.'

'Result!' Scott murmured under his breath as he hid behind the door. All he had to do was follow and, with any luck, the dreadlocked man would lead him to Rosie and Dr Armitage.

—

Meanwhile, Emily and Jack were having a minor dispute. They'd made it to a back door, where Drift had come running up to meet them. They'd entered the mansion, crossed a laundry room and found themselves hurrying along a corridor.

When Emily spotted an open door into a large office, she voted they make a detour. 'We could gather loads of evidence about what these guys are up to …'

Jack disagreed. 'We just need to find Rosie and her gran and get out.'

'I just need five minutes!'

Jack started to protest but Emily was already inside the office. 'You and Drift keep watch, OK?'

Drift's ears drooped; he was with Jack on this one.

Jack sighed. 'Five minutes, that's all!'

Emily pulled on her latex gloves to avoid leaving fingerprints. She moved quickly from desk to computer to filing cabinet, pulling open drawers, riffling through piles of paper, scanning for incriminating evidence – forged documents, details of smuggled goods, false accounts …

But to her great disappointment, everything seemed perfectly in order.

Emily stood in the middle of the room. Jack and Drift were both making move-it faces at her. Had she got it all wrong? Was Peter Barrington just an ordinary businessman running an ordinary business selling ordinary mobile-phone parts, after all?

But if the business was all above-board, why had Motorbike Man brought the man with the broken leg here to Barrington Towers? And why were they holding Dr Armitage and Rosie hostage? Not to mention the guns and the bag full of diamonds and fifty-pound notes. None of that was *ordinary*!

Emily was about to give up and leave when she noticed a shaft of sunlight shining on a metal filing cabinet against the back wall, showing up the smudges of old fingerprints. The fingerprints weren't along the tops of the drawers. They were all on the sides, as if people had gripped the cabinet to move it. She looked at the floor. A faint scuff-mark formed an arc from the corner of the cabinet.

'Quick!' she whispered to Jack. 'Come and give me a hand.'

Jack looked up and down the corridor. He shook his head frantically, but he knew there was no point.

They took one side each and tugged.

The filing cabinet swung out from the wall.

'*I knew it!*' Emily breathed. There was a door hidden behind the cabinet. She pulled it open and peeped inside. More desks, computers, filing cabinets and photocopiers: there was a whole other secret office behind the wall! She picked a desk at random and opened a drawer to reveal a stack of passports. They were clearly all false; some of them bore the same name but different photos, others had the same photo but different names.

Emily was in paradise!

She found a pile of certificates next to the photocopier that said they guaranteed that a diamond had not come from a war zone. She found stamps with the words *Approved by Amsterdam Customs* ready to be inked and added to the certificates. She found diagrams showing how to hide diamonds inside mobile phones . . .

This was where the *real* business of Barrington Towers was done!

Emily took out her phone and started snapping photographs.

She could hear Jack and Drift hopping from foot to foot and paw to paw behind her. They'd been much longer than five minutes. *Just one more photo* . . . but then she pulled open a drawer to see trays and trays of huge sparkling diamonds. 'Wow! Look at this!' she called.

Jack hurried across the secret office and stared over her shoulder in amazement.

Drift pricked up his ears and gave a soft warning bark, but it was too late.

'What have we got here, then?'

Emily spun round. The voice came from a burly man with flames tattooed all over his bald scalp. He was standing right behind Jack. As he spoke he grabbed Jack's shoulder. Emily noticed his knuckles were hairy and tattooed with the words *Bad News*.

'The boss will be *very* interested to hear about this!' Flame Head held out his hand to Emily. 'Give me that phone you were trying to sneak into your bag.'

Emily had no choice but to drop her mobile – and all her lovely evidence – into the man's beefy palm.

Eighteen

The Boss's Orders

While Jack and Emily were being frog-marched out of the office, Scott was crouching behind a huge vase of emerald-green bamboo stems. He'd managed to tail the dreadlocked henchman all the way from the home cinema, up three flights of stairs and along a corridor without being seen. Now his target had disappeared inside a room.

Through the crack in the door, Scott could see that

a meeting was in progress. The dreadlocked man had joined several people, who were sitting round a long glass-topped table, smoking cigarettes and drinking coffee.

A large grey-haired man, in a pink and blue checked golf jumper that was stretched to bursting point over his bulbous stomach, was sitting at one end of the table giving out orders. 'Kristal, you're on the first flight to Johannesburg on Monday. The usual contact will meet you at the airport.' He puffed on a fat cigar and slid a folder along the table to a middle-aged woman in a white velvet tracksuit, her blonde hair puffed into a candyfloss swirl. 'Here are your travel papers and the certificates you'll need to get through customs.' The woman nodded and slipped the documents into a leopardskin handbag, her diamond bracelets clinking as they slid down her wrist.

The large man blew out a smoke ring and waved his cigar at another member of the group. 'Sammy! Get to Amsterdam and sort out that shipment from Angola.'

The cigar puffer must be Peter Barrington, Scott thought, straining his left eyeball for a better view through the crack in the door. *The boss!*

Suddenly Barrington thumped the table. 'Now, will *somebody* tell me what exactly is going on with these aeroplane drops over Castle Key? Has Gert's broken leg been attended to?'

The dreadlocked man nodded. 'Yes, boss. We've got our usual doctor with him now.'

Barrington frowned and examined the end of his cigar. 'This whole Castle Key operation is going pear-shaped. I should never have allowed it.'

'Flying those light aircraft in low and slow over the moors and dropping the bags down for Steve to pick up worked pretty well the first two nights ...' the woman in the white tracksuit said.

At last! Scott thought. He finally had the answer to what had really caused the phantom lights. They belonged to the smugglers' delivery plane. And the light Jack had seen dancing beneath the other lights must have been Steve – aka Motorbike Man – signalling with his torch as he waited on the ground to collect the bags of diamonds.

'That's not good enough!' the boss growled. 'The third drop was a disaster! Has the missing bag turned up yet?'

The woman in the white tracksuit fiddled nervously with her bangles. 'No, Steve swears it's still lost, lying out on the moor somewhere. Apparently, the plane couldn't get in low enough because of the wind conditions.'

'I'll deal with Steve later.' Barrington leaned back in his chair. 'Where are the two prisoners – the local doctor and her granddaughter?'

The man with the dreadlocks cleared his throat. 'We're holding them in one of the storerooms downstairs.'

Barrington crushed his cigar out in a glittering gold ashtray. 'Fetch them up here immediately. I'm sure they know something about the missing diamonds. And if they do, believe me, I'll *persuade* them to tell me.'

The way Barrington kept grinding that cigar stub into the ashtray long after it was out made Scott's blood run cold. Something told him that the boss's idea of *persuasion* didn't involve saying *please, pretty please* over a nice cup of tea.

Scott knew he had to find Rosie and Dr Armitage before the boss got hold of them.

He shrank back behind the bamboo and prepared to follow the dreadlocked man once again.

—

Meanwhile, Jack, Emily and Drift were being bundled into a small room crowded with spare furniture. Rosie and Dr Armitage were already there, perched side by side on a small table. A bored-looking man was sitting on a white satin sofa keeping guard.

Rosie and her gran both looked up as the door opened. Their mouths fell open in shock as they saw the new arrivals.

'But how did you—' Rosie began, but she was silenced by a bark of 'Shut it!' from their guard.

Flame Head pushed Emily and Jack down onto a pile of rugs. Then he knocked knuckles with the other guard. 'I'll stay and watch them for a bit,' he told him. 'Go and get something to eat.'

Drift sat at Emily's side with his head on her lap, wondering what they were doing in this strange place and why everyone smelled so scared.

Flame Head sank down on the sofa, hunched over his phone and started checking his messages.

Could we overpower him? Jack wondered. It was four against one, after all. But the guy with the headful of fiery tattoos clearly put in some serious time in the gym; enormous biceps bulged like balloons from his black sleeveless vest. And then there was the large gun resting on the sofa cushion only millimetres from his hip.

Jack watched a wasp buzz in through the window. Flame Head glanced up at it. He looked back at his phone, but every time the wasp moved he eyed it nervously. *Looks like he feels the same way about wasps as I do about spiders*, Jack thought. The wasp landed on the man's bare shoulder. Flame Head jumped out of his skin.

Suddenly Jack had an idea. 'Keep still!' he screamed, staring at the yellow and black wasp – his eyes wide as if in terror. 'It's one of those African Hornet Wasps. If they sting you ...' he gulped and let his voice tail off as if the words were too terrible to say out loud.

'If they sting you, *what*?' Flame Head demanded. 'Is it painful?'

'Agony!' Jack said. 'I saw it on that TV programme – *World's Deadliest Insects*. It's like your bones are melting. Then the toxins eat into your brain. You end up paralysed.'

'Yeah, right! If there were wasps that dangerous in Cornwall, I'd have heard of them.' Flame Head didn't sound too sure though. He spoke through clenched teeth and didn't move a muscle.

'It's an *alien* species,' Jack improvised. 'Like grey squirrels. These wasps have only just started invading this summer. They came in banana crates from Africa. It's been on all the news programmes.'

Drift looked up at Jack. Why was he talking about squirrels *again*?

'That's right!' Emily chipped in, seeing what Jack was up to. 'I saw that programme too.' She shuddered. 'That poor man with the ... well, I won't go into details. You'd better let one of us try to shoo it off your arm for you.'

Flame Head narrowed his eyes. 'How do I know you won't just let it sting me so you can get away?'

Annoyingly, Jack thought, Flame Head wasn't quite as dumb as he looked – which was pretty dumb, since his head was permanently on fire.

'If you let me have my medical bag,' Dr Armitage said, 'I've got a dose of the antidote. We've had government advice that all doctors in this area should start carrying the African Hornet Wasp antidote in case of emergency, but it has to be given within thirty seconds of a sting to work.'

Jack shot the doctor an admiring glance. *Genius!* he thought. If he didn't know he'd invented the deadly African Hornet Wasp himself just ten seconds ago he'd have believed every word of it!

'Go on then!' Flame Head hissed. Beads of sweat were forming on his fiery scalp. 'But keep your hands where I can see them.'

Dr Armitage walked across the room with her hands up and stooped to pick up her old brown leather bag.

'Tip it out on the floor so I can see you haven't got a gun in there,' Flame Head ordered.

'Of course I haven't got a gun!' Dr Armitage fired back. 'I'm a doctor, not an armed thug. Now do you want me to help you or not?' She picked out a frighteningly large syringe and began to fill it from a small glass bottle.

'Hurry up!' Flame Head muttered. 'I can't keep still much longer.'

At last Dr Armitage had filled the syringe. She stood close to the flame-tattooed man. 'Right. Jack, you come and shoo the wasp away,' she instructed. 'I'm ready to give the antidote if it's needed.'

Jack suspected Dr Armitage was starting to enjoy herself. 'On a count of three,' she said. 'One, two ...'

Jack didn't wait for *three*! He whacked the guard's shoulder with a cushion – deliberately missing the wasp, of course!

At exactly the same moment, Dr Armitage thrust the needle of the syringe into the man's meaty bicep.

Jack made a grab for the gun, but Flame Head got there first. He picked it up, pointed it at Jack and squeezed the trigger.

Jack sensed a flash of movement. Then he felt the impact and collapsed in a heap.

I've been shot! Jack thought. *I'm going to die!*

Then he realized he wasn't dead – or even injured. The movement had been Rosie's foot. She'd leaped across the room and karate-kicked the gun out of the man's hand. It flew across the room and slid under a bookcase. The impact he'd felt was Emily. She'd thrown herself at Jack, knocking him to the floor and out of the line of fire.

Jack looked up from beneath Emily's armpit.

Drift was attacking Flame Head's ankles.

Flame Head's eyes bulged. He gurgled and rocked forwards for a moment, as if to push Drift away. Then he fell back against the sofa.

'We've *killed* him!' Jack gasped.

'No. Just a hefty shot of morphine,' Dr Armitage said. 'He'll be out for a while.' She paused and grinned. 'You can't be too careful with African Hornet Wasps.' She reached down and shook Jack by the hand. 'Jolly good work!'

Emily stood up and pulled Jack to his feet.

'Cheers for the ninja rescue routine,' Jack told Emily

and Rosie. 'You too, Drift!' he added, stooping to ruffle Drift's fur. 'Obviously, I had it all under control, but thanks anyway.'

'Of course, you did!' the girls laughed.

But suddenly Emily was serious again. 'Come on! Let's get out of here. Another guard could turn up any second.'

But it was already too late. They were only halfway to the door when it flew open and a mean-looking man with close-set eyes and long dreadlocks stepped into the room.

Jack, Emily, Rosie and Dr Armitage all stopped in their tracks and stared in dismay. How could this happen? After all that work they were back to square one!

But just when it seemed it was all over, the dreadlocked man gave a small gasp of surprise and staggered forwards before crumpling to his knees and keeling over to land face-down on the carpet.

'What …' Jack gulped.

Scott was standing in the doorway with a pool cue clutched in both hands.

Dr Armitage hurried to the pole-axed henchman's side and checked his pulse. She looked up at Scott. 'You've knocked him out cold!'

Emily ran to Scott. 'What's going on?'

Scott was still clutching the pool cue so tightly his knuckles were white. 'The boss thinks we've stolen his delivery of diamonds . . .'

'How do you know?' Jack asked.

Scott shook his head. 'Long story but, believe me, we don't want to be caught!'

Emily glanced at the comatose henchmen. 'That's two down! How many more are there?'

'Loads!' Scott groaned. 'But most of them are watching the football. If we can get out before the end of the match we might just stand a chance.'

Nineteen

Death-defying Rescue Missions

Scott looked out of the door. The coast was clear. He beckoned to Jack, Emily, Rosie and Dr Armitage. They all tiptoed out and made their way along the corridor, with Drift padding along at Emily's heels.

They had just reached the top of the stairs when they heard voices. 'The boss just called. Said he'd sent Larry to fetch the doctor and the girl but he's not come back.

157

Not answering his radio either. He wants us to go and check it out.'

'Typical!' a second voice grumbled. 'If I miss the end of the match there'll be trouble!'

Scott looked over his shoulder. Two of the men he'd seen in the home cinema were coming towards them. 'Quick, down the stairs!' he whispered.

But they'd been spotted. The men started to run after them.

Jack turned to pull Rosie along with him but, to his horror, she was no longer right behind him. She'd tripped. The men were almost upon her. Jack ran back, grabbed her hand and dragged her out of their reach. Together they ran to the nearest door, dived through it and slammed it behind them.

Jack looked round. They were in a fancy bedroom, all decked out in black and white. Rosie was already tugging a dressing table across the thick white carpet. Jack helped her push it up to the door and they leaned against it, panting.

Jack knew the dressing table wouldn't hold for long. He could already feel it juddering beneath him as the men kicked on the other side of the door. There had to be another way out. He pointed at the French doors that led out onto a balcony on the other side of the room. 'That's our only chance!'

'OK. Let's do it!' Rosie said, dashing across the room.

Jack joined her, rattling the handle and shoving so

hard with his shoulder that the glass doors shattered and showered the friends with fragments as they flew open. Behind them, Jack heard the dressing table topple over and the mirror smash, as one of the guards burst through the door.

Rosie was leaning over the railing of the balcony. 'It's too far to jump!' she cried.

Jack ran to her side. She was right. They were on the second floor – so high up that they were level with the bright green leaves of the palm trees. Jack looked down. The patio below was made of crazy paving. It would make a bone-breaking landing. The swimming pool was off to one side. The turquoise water sparkled invitingly, but it was too far to jump. There weren't even any vines or drainpipes to climb down.

Jack could hear the man storming across the bedroom now. He was almost at the French doors. Suddenly he knew what they had to do. It was crazy, it probably wouldn't work, but there was no other option!

'Use the palm trees!' he shouted, climbing onto the balcony railing and pulling Rosie up beside him.

'What do you mean?' Rosie gasped.

'Like this!' Jack cried, launching himself off the railing towards the cluster of long green leaves. For a moment he was flying through the air. Then he felt the leaves and clung on for all he was worth, even though the sharp edges tore at his fingers. He felt a strange slow-motion lurch as the thin trunk bent under

159

his weight like a giant pole-vaulting pole. It gathered speed as it swung him down towards the patio. Jack let go, landing heavily and rolling onto his shoulder. Freed of its load, the palm tree snapped upright again with a *whoosh*.

Jack looked up to see Rosie clinging on to the next palm tree along, her legs flying out as it whipped her through the air towards him. She let go just in time and tumbled to the ground next to Jack as the tree began to spring back.

'Wow!' Rosie laughed as Jack pulled her to her feet. 'Where did you learn that trick? It was like something out of one of those classic Chinese martial arts films!'

Jack grinned. He didn't tell Rosie that the only martial arts film he'd seen was *Kung Fu Panda*.

They ran for the gate.

Scott, Emily, Dr Armitage and Drift hurtled down two flights of stairs, raced across the hall and threw open the front door.

Scott cursed as he looked out. The big black electric gates were closed, of course! He checked the control panel on the wall. There was a button marked OPEN GATES. He could press it, but by the time they got to the end of the long drive, the gates would have shut again. There had to be some way of programming the device to add a delay, but there was no time to figure that out. One of the henchmen was clattering down the stairs and would be upon them any second.

Emily was fishing in her bag. 'I've got some Blu-Tack. If we could just stick down the button . . . Where is it?'

Suddenly Scott had a better idea. The chewing gum Emily had given him had lost its taste long ago but he hadn't had a chance to get rid of it. He spat it out, pressed down the button and stuck the chewing gum over it. 'Hurry!' Scott yelled, as they ran down the marble steps. The gates were swishing open but he knew the chewing gum wouldn't hold that button down for long.

'Wait!' Dr Armitage cried, skidding to a halt in the middle of the drive. 'Where's Rosie?'

Scott spun round. His knees almost gave way beneath him. Rosie was missing. And so was Jack!

Emily was horrified. 'But they were right behind us!'

'We'll have to go back for them!' Dr Armitage panted.

But suddenly Drift barked in the direction of two figures running towards them across the lawn.

'It's Jack and Rosie!' Emily cried.

There was no time to ask where they'd been or how they'd escaped. Gang members were running out of the house and heading their way like a swarm of angry bees.

'Quick!' Scott yelled, as Jack and Rosie drew closer. 'The gates are closing!'

They all began to run. Jack and Rosie were the last to make it. The two gates were sliding rapidly together. *Someone in the house must have pressed the Emergency High-Speed Close button or something*, Jack thought. There was barely a shoulder-width between them now. He pushed Rosie through. Then he dived, twisting sideways as he went, just making it through the gap.

Jack landed in a heap on top of Scott, Emily, Drift, Dr Armitage and Rosie. He sat up, laughing with relief at their narrow escape. But then he noticed his sock. One of his trainers had come off as he jumped. He could see it lying just on the other side of the gates, which had now almost met in the middle. *No way!* he thought. These were his favourite trainers. He'd only had them since the beginning of the holiday. It was just like when Indiana Jones rolled under the closing gate and his hat fell off. *Did Indy leave his trusty hat behind? No, of course not! He reached back with seconds to spare …*

Jack thrust his arm through the gap and grabbed his trainer.

'Agghh!' he yelled, as the gates snapped shut on his hand like crocodile jaws.

Just in time, Scott grasped Jack's arm and pulled him free.

Jack looked down at his hand. It was bright red and throbbing like mad. He was pretty sure that hadn't happened to Indiana Jones.

But at least he had his trainer!

The escape party stopped at the end of the beach, gasping for breath. They had run down the road and through the funfair, trying to lose themselves in the crowds in case any of the men from Barrington Towers had followed them out. After weaving through queues for the dodgems and the rollercoaster and taking a short cut through the ghost train, they felt it safe to stop at last.

Rosie and her gran hugged each other, tears running down their faces.

'I don't know how you kids found me,' Dr Armitage gulped, 'but well done!'

Scott sank down onto the warm sand. 'The first thing we need is ...'

'... massive triple-scoop ice creams all round,' Jack finished for him. 'Death-defying rescue missions are hungry work!'

'No, that's the *second* thing,' Scott laughed. 'First, we have to call the police and tell them there's a diamond smuggling operation running out of Barrington Towers.'

'That's right,' Emily agreed. 'Now that Dr Armitage

and Rosie are out of there, we don't have to worry about them being harmed.'

'We need to be quick,' Scott went on. 'As soon as Peter Barrington realizes that we've escaped, he'll know that we could report him at any moment so he'll be busy destroying all the evidence.'

Rosie nodded. 'And then it will just be our word against his.'

Jack grinned. 'Ah, but we've also got Em's photos of all the dodgy forged passports and certificates that we found in the hidden office.' But then his face fell. 'Oh, no! I forgot, Flame Head took Emily's phone away.'

'Ta da!' Emily declared and pulled her phone out of her bag with a flourish.

Jack stared at her. 'How did you get it back?'

'I sneaked it out of his pocket when he was unconscious on the sofa ... just before Scott turned up and bopped the other guard on the head.'

'Where did you get that pool cue, by the way?' Jack asked Scott.

'Games room,' Scott said with a grin. 'Em's not the only one who can pinch things!'

Emily dialled Carrickstowe Police Station and asked to speak to Detective Inspector Hassan. She thought it would be a challenge to convince him that a so-called respectable businessman was running a diamond smuggling operation but, to her surprise, the inspector believed her straight away.

'We've suspected Peter Barrington was up to something for a long time,' he said. 'This is just the evidence we need to go in and raid Barrington Towers. I'm sending a special unit round there now!'

'Now, can we get those ice creams?' Jack asked as Emily ended the call.

'My treat!' Dr Armitage laughed, taking Jack by the arm and striding towards the ice-cream van. 'Do you think there is such a thing as a *quadruple* scoop? We'll get some ice for that hand you trapped in the gate, too!'

As he took his first lick of his vanilla, chocolate, strawberry and raspberry ripple ice cream (with sauce and sprinkles, of course), Jack glimpsed a convoy of police cars speeding down the seafront road towards Barrington Towers.

~

The friends slept late the following morning, then met at Dotty's Tea Rooms for lunch to celebrate the success of Operation Phantom Lights.

Everything had turned out perfectly. Jack's mysterious 'alien' lights on the moors had turned out to be the smugglers' plane flying in low to drop bags of money and diamonds. Dr Armitage was safely back home with Rosie and her mum. And D. I. Hassan had called earlier in the morning to say that the police raid had been a success. They'd rounded up and arrested everyone at

Barrington Towers, plus a number of others at another nearby address used by the gang.

Emily had spent the previous evening writing up the investigation in her notebook. She couldn't wait to hand over her case notes and photos of the evidence when she went with Scott and Jack to give their statements at the police station.

It seemed the case was closed.

But there was just *one* mystery that remained unsolved.

The police had found Peter Barrington. They'd found Gert with the broken leg, Hank with the flame-tattooed head, Larry with the dreadlocks, Kristal, the woman in the white velvet tracksuit, and all the other gangmembers the friends had encountered.

But they hadn't found a short, slim man called Steve, with a big beard and small feet.

It seemed Motorbike Man had vanished into thin air.

Twenty

Lost and Found

'Motorbike Man was definitely at Barrington Towers,' Scott said. 'I saw him in the games room.'

'And his hire car was still parked near the garage when we left,' Jack added.

'So how come the police didn't find him?' Emily sighed. Motorbike Man's disappearance was really bugging her! She was sure he was the vital link between the diamond smuggling operation and Castle Key. Until he showed up, there were still unanswered questions.

And Emily hated unanswered questions!

She was chewing on her straw, pondering the problem, as Dotty arrived at the table with their food.

Jack had ordered the Super Special with extra pineapple and chilli again. He hoped he'd get to eat it this time! Scott was having a mega-burger. It was a double celebration, after all. Chelsea had won yesterday's match, beating Ajax on penalties!

'Are you feeling better now?' Emily asked Dotty, as Dotty handed her a margherita pizza.

Dotty looked puzzled. 'Sorry, what?'

Jack reached for the ketchup. 'Mrs White said you had the flu.'

'Oh, yes, thank you. I'm fine now.'

But she didn't *look* fine, Emily thought, as she watched Dotty refilling the coffee machine behind the counter. Emily had known Dotty for years. She'd never seen her look so miserable. There were hollows under her cheekbones and panda rings around her eyes. Emily wasn't exactly an expert on personal grooming, but Dotty's red and white summer dress looked as if it had been fished out of the laundry basket, her long blonde hair hadn't seen a hairbrush for days and her chin was breaking out in a rash. When she put down the coffee pot to answer the phone she looked as though she were about to burst into tears. Was it trouble with her boyfriend? Emily wondered. She wished there was a way she could help.

A few minutes later Dotty ended her call. She brushed tears from her eyes with the back of her hand and hurried across to clear the friends' table. 'I'm sorry to hurry you,' she said, 'but I'm going to have to close the café for a while. I've got to go out. A family emergency.'

'No problem,' Jack said, draining the last of his Coke. He leaned back and patted his stomach. 'Great pizza! Thanks!'

Emily took the glasses over to the counter and helped Dotty stack them in the dishwasher.

Dotty began pulling a black leather jacket on over her dress. 'Oh, dash it!' she muttered. 'I've lost a button!' She started to glance around on the floor.

Emily looked up from the dishwasher. 'I'll help you find it. What does it look like?'

Dotty smiled weakly and held out her arm to show Emily one of the buttons on the cuff of the jacket. 'Thanks, but don't worry. I don't know when it came off.'

But Emily was still gazing at the little silver stud button on the jacket. She was sure she'd seen one just like it not so long ago. Then she remembered. It was the same as the one she'd found on the lavender hedge outside Dr Armitage's house. She ran back to her bag and took out the little plastic evidence pouch.

She couldn't help feeling disappointed that the button hadn't turned out to come from Motorbike Man's jacket and wouldn't provide a vital clue in the diamond smuggling case, but at least it might cheer Dotty up a bit to get it back. She held it out on her palm. 'Here it is,' she said. 'I found it the other day.'

Dotty smiled as she picked it up. 'Thanks, Emily. Where was it?'

'Just outside Dr Armitage's house in Tregower …' Emily's words tailed off. For some reason, Dotty's face – already pale – had suddenly drained of colour, as if someone had walked over her grave. Even the black rings under her eyes had turned grey. Her hand shook as she slid the button into her pocket. She swallowed hard and tried to hide it under a breezy smile, but something had given her a fright. *It was when I mentioned Dr Armitage's house*, Emily thought.

'Oh, yes, of course,' Dotty said in a bright voice. 'I remember now. I was there the other day. Er, Tuesday, or was it Wednesday? I'm not sure. I had an appointment to see Dr Armitage.' Dotty looked down, making a big show of rummaging for her car keys in her handbag. 'Yes, that's right. It was about this terrible flu I've had …'

Emily smiled and nodded. Why was Dotty babbling? According to *Lie Detection: Theory and Methods*, giving far too much information was a sure sign of lying. But why would Dotty lie about something as innocent as going to the doctor about flu?

Dotty jangled her keys. 'Ah, here we are. Must dash. I'll see you out and lock up.' She held open the door of the café for the friends to leave.

Emily filed out after Scott and Jack and Drift. She knew something was wrong with Dotty's story. She couldn't put her finger on it at first but, as Dotty turned the key in the lock of the door behind them, it came to her. *The wrong door!* If Dotty had had an appointment to see Dr Armitage she'd have gone to the surgery door – the glossy black one with the brass plaque next to it. But Emily had found the button on the path outside the other door – the one the family use.

The door that you'd knock on if you needed to wake the doctor in the middle of the night!

Suddenly, Emily felt cold fingers of dread wrap themselves around her heart. She had a horrible feeling she knew *exactly* why the police hadn't found Motorbike Man at Barrington Towers.

~

As soon as they were standing outside the café and Dotty was heading off down the seafront to the spot where her car was parked, Emily grabbed Scott and Jack by the arms. She was in such a state of shock she could hardly get the words out. 'Dotty was the one who called at Dr Armitage's house the night she disappeared,' she whispered. 'I found the missing button from her jacket on the path there.'

Scott stared at Emily. 'What? You think Dotty was with Motorbike Man when the diamond smuggling drop went wrong and the parachute guy was injured?'

'But why would she cover up for him?' Jack asked.

Emily shook her head. 'I don't think Dotty was *with* Motorbike Man. I think Dotty *is* Motorbike Man!'

Twenty-one

A Long Story

Jack watched Dotty walk down the seafront towards her red Mini. Her long blonde plait hung down the back of her leather jacket and her dress swished as she walked. 'I may not be Einstein,' he snorted, 'but even I know that Dotty isn't a man!'

But Scott looked from Emily to Dotty and back to Emily. He was thinking so hard Jack could almost hear the cogs turning in his brain. 'False beard?' he said slowly. 'And a wig?'

Emily nodded. 'The glue from the beard would explain the rash on her chin.'

'Motorbike Man *was* short and slim, I suppose.' But then Scott laughed and shook his head. 'No, it's crazy! There must be millions of short, slim men with beards out there …'

'I noticed he had very small feet for a man,' Emily pointed out. 'That's not exactly common.'

Scott shrugged. He was about to argue when he thought of something else. 'It would explain why he mumbled so badly, I suppose, if it were Dotty trying to disguise her voice. And the dodgy London accent.'

Emily nodded. 'And remember how Drift ran up to Motorbike Man on the moors. He wasn't fooled by a false beard.' Emily gave Drift a hug. 'You *knew* it was Dotty all along, didn't you?'

'Hello!' Jack chimed in, staring at Emily and Scott as if they had totally lost their marbles. 'Reality check here! This is our *friend*, Dotty, we're talking about. The same Dotty who gives us extra-large pizzas and free ice creams. You're not seriously saying she's a secret diamond smuggler, are you?'

Emily didn't reply. She shaded her eyes against the sun and watched Dotty open the door of her Mini.

'And anyway,' Jack went on, 'how could Dotty have been running around smuggling diamonds and abducting grannies when she's been in bed with flu all week?' But suddenly he hesitated, remembering something the Viking Biker had said in the café yesterday. He'd called at Dotty's flat and *she wasn't there*! 'Well, she might have been lying about the flu, I suppose,' Jack muttered.

The three friends looked at each other. They all knew it sounded crazy but evidence was evidence!

Dotty's little red Mini was pulling away from the kerb. Without another word, they all ran out in front of it, waving their arms for Dotty to stop. She braked and wound down the window. 'What's wrong?' she asked. 'Did you leave something in the café?'

Emily poked her head in through the window. 'What size are your feet?'

Dotty laughed. 'Six and a half. Why?'

'What do you know about diamond smuggling?' Scott asked, leaning over Emily's shoulder.

'I don't know what you're talking about,' Dotty said.

'We know that you disguised yourself as a man,' Emily told her.

'With a false beard,' Scott added.

'And motorbike gear,' Jack said, pushing Scott aside to get a look in. He still didn't believe it was true, but the motorbike helmet on the passenger seat of the Mini was hard to ignore.

'I don't even ride a motorbike ...' Dotty stammered.

Emily looked pointedly at the helmet.

'That's not mine!' Dotty blustered. 'It belongs to, er ...'

'Why did you pick the name Steve?' Scott cut in.

'I just went for something ordinary ...' Dotty snapped her mouth shut as she realized she'd given herself away. Her head sank to the steering wheel. When she looked up, tears were running down her face. 'I'm sorry,' she sobbed. 'I had no choice ...'

—

Emily didn't know whether to be furious with Dotty for deceiving them or sorry for her. One thing she did know; she needed to hear the whole story. 'Let's go back into the café,' she said. 'We'll make you a cup of tea.'

Dotty let herself be led inside and seated at a table. She blew her nose on a napkin. 'I only did it to save my brother's life,' she sniffled. 'Aidan's ten years younger than me. He was a great kid but a bit of a joker at school, always getting in trouble.'

Jack passed her a mug of tea. He liked this Aidan guy already. 'What kind of trouble?' he asked.

Dotty curled both hands around the mug as if for warmth, even though the midday sun was beating through the windows. 'When Aidan wasn't much older than you guys he fell in with a crowd of older boys. They pretended to be his friends but they were just taking advantage of him. They got him shoplifting and stealing cars and all sorts. They took his money and he ran up all kinds of debt. I bailed him out over and over again, but then he got mixed up with the Barrington gang. They told him they'd pay off his debts if he travelled to Amsterdam and smuggled diamonds back inside fake mobile phones, but they didn't keep their word, of course. They just got him to do bigger and bigger jobs. The trouble was, he wasn't very good at it.'

'What happened?' Emily asked.

'He was almost caught. The customs officials got suspicious so the gang had to stop using that route. Aidan called me a few weeks ago in a terrible state. He said that the boss had told him he had to find someone to help with this new plan they'd come up with to fly the diamonds in to Castle Key and drop them over the moors. The planes are so small and fly so low that they aren't picked up by air traffic control. They needed someone on the ground who knew the island well.'

Dotty's voice dropped to a whisper. 'Aidan said they'd kill him if he didn't set this operation up for them. I didn't want to break the law,' she sobbed, 'and I hated what Barrington was doing. He's not just avoiding paying taxes by smuggling the diamonds. Those diamonds are mined in countries where wars are going on and the profits are used to buy weapons. That's why it's illegal to bring them into this country.' Dotty gulped back her tears. 'I only did it to save my brother's life.'

'What did you have to do?' Scott asked.

Dotty sipped her tea. 'It was only going to be three drops – just until the gang could go back to using their usual smuggling route. I got a message to tell me when the plane would fly over. I had to wait on the moor, signal my location with a torch, pick up the bag that was dropped from the plane and then hand it over at a secret meeting place in Carrickstowe. The Barrington gang lent me the motorbike to use so that my car wouldn't be recognized. The diamonds and the cash were all packed in pizza boxes and flasks, so that if anyone stopped me it would look like I was making a delivery.'

Jack swallowed a lump in his throat. He could understand why Dotty had agreed to help the smugglers to save her hopeless brother's life. That was just how it worked with brothers. He'd been ready to climb into a perilous ravine without ropes to save Scott, after all, and Scott was the most annoying brother ever! But there was one thing he *didn't* get. 'Why did you dress up as a man?'

'I didn't want the gang to know who I was. Otherwise they'd be able to blackmail me into working for them again any time they wanted, just by threatening to reveal that I'd been part of their diamond smuggling racket!'

'That makes sense,' Emily said. 'This way Steve the Motorbike Man could disappear at the end of the operation and nobody could connect him to you.'

Dotty gave a grim nod.

'But something went wrong on the third drop?' Scott asked.

'The plane was having trouble flying low enough. They dropped the bag but it landed too far away for me to see. It must have rolled away and I couldn't find it.' Dotty gazed into her mug, as if seeing the events play out in front of her eyes again. 'I radioed up to tell them the problem. The co-pilot, Gert, parachuted down to help me look for it, but he landed badly and hurt his leg. It was terrible. He was screaming. I dragged him to the pillbox nearby. I wanted to call an ambulance but he wouldn't let me.'

'So you went to Tregower and fetched Dr Armitage to help?' Emily asked.

'That's right. I didn't know Gert was going to hold her prisoner at gunpoint the minute she got there!' Dotty shook her head. 'It's all been a nightmare. I was going back and forth to the pillbox to take food and water for Gert and Dr Armitage. I pretended to be ill to explain why I wasn't at the café. I've been leading a double life, changing into Steve and back again. I haven't slept for weeks with all the worry. And then Rosie turned up at the pillbox too. I felt terrible. I really didn't mean anything bad to happen to anyone.'

'I know you didn't,' Scott said gently. 'You tried to talk the guy with the broken leg into letting Rosie and her gran go.'

Dotty jerked her head up and stared at him. 'How do you know that?'

'It's a long story,' Scott said. 'Let's just say we had you – or rather, *Steve* – under observation …'

Dotty nodded. She'd known the friends long enough to know about their investigations. 'When I first heard you talking about the strange lights on the moors I knew it must be the smugglers' plane you'd seen. I tried to warn you away with all those stories about evil piskies. I didn't want you to get mixed up in it.' She managed a weak smile. 'I should have known you three wouldn't take any notice!'

'It was us who rescued Dr Armitage and Rosie and called the police to Barrington Towers,' Jack said proudly.

'I wondered who'd tipped the police off,' Dotty said. 'I was sitting in the games room – Barrington's men had told me to wait there until I was summoned – when I heard the police arrive. I quickly changed out of my Steve disguise and ran to the front door. I'd seen a *Dotty's Pizza* box lying around in the games room so I grabbed it on the way and pretended I'd just turned up to deliver a Super Special. Luckily, one of the policemen was a regular customer here at the café so he recognized me – as Dotty, not Steve, of course. He never thought to doubt my story and he let me walk away. I got the bus home!'

'So what are you going to do now?' Emily asked.

'First I'm going to the police station to see Aidan. The police arrested him at one of the other properties owned by the Barringtons. That's who was on the phone just now.'

'We were about to go to the police station too,' Scott said, 'to give our statements.'

Dotty blew her nose on a paper napkin. 'I know you're good kids. You always tell the truth so you'll have no choice but to turn me in.' She gazed around the café, her eyes swimming with tears. 'I've worked so hard to build this place up. It'll break my heart to lose it.'

Emily looked at Scott and Scott looked at Jack. They all nodded in unspoken agreement.

'It's OK,' Scott said at last. 'We won't tell them about you. The real criminals have all been caught and that's what matters.' He paused and then added, 'As long as you swear you won't get mixed up with any more criminal activities.'

Dotty nodded seriously. 'Of course.' She gave a weak smile. 'I'd never had as much as a speeding fine before all this. My life of crime is *definitely* over.'

'That's settled then,' Emily said. 'Steve the mysterious Motorbike Man can just remain on the police Most Wanted list forever!'

'And anyway,' Jack added, 'what would we do without Dotty's Tea Rooms? Nobody makes pizza like you do!'

Dotty laughed, then cried, then hugged them all. But

suddenly she looked sad again. 'The only problem is that Peter Barrington still thinks "Steve" stole the bag of cash and diamonds that we lost on the last drop. Until it turns up, the gang will believe that Steve and Aidan double-crossed them. I know many of them will be in prison after this but they'll still have contacts on the outside. Aidan won't be safe until I find that missing bag, but I've searched and searched the moors . . .'

The bag! Jack thought. He could hardly believe that in all the commotion of the rescue mission he'd forgotten hiding it in the hollow tree. He jumped out of his seat. 'We know where it is!'

Dotty gaped at Jack. 'Really?'

Scott nodded. 'We'll tell the police how we found it and we can take them to the bag.'

'Then the police can tell the Barrington gang that Steve didn't steal it,' Emily said.

'And,' Jack put in, 'your brother will be safe!'

'Thank you!' Dotty gasped, hugging them all again. Then she ran to the door. 'Come on! If you don't mind all squeezing into the Mini, I'll give you a lift to the police station.'

Twenty-two

Good News

'Ta da!' Jack cried, sweeping his arms open like a magician introducing his next spellbinding trick.

A small crowd had gathered around the old willow tree to witness the retrieval of the bag of diamonds and money. Emily, Scott and Drift were there, of course, along with Detective Inspector Hassan, two uniformed officers and the police photographer.

Jack stepped inside the enormous hollow trunk

and reached into the cavity in the gnarled bark where he'd tucked the bag out of sight. He felt around under the dry leaves and twigs. 'Just in here somewhere,' he said, still smiling, although he was starting to wonder whether this was the right hole. He tried the one above. There was nothing there either. He looked round to see D. I. Hassan staring down at him. Jack could tell by the twitching of his luxuriant black moustache that the inspector was not amused.

'Someone must have moved it,' Jack mumbled.

Scott rolled his eyes. 'Like who? Squirrels?'

Jack felt hot, then cold. He thought he might be sick. Everyone was looking at him. Millions of pounds of cash and diamonds had gone missing and it was all his fault.

'Is this some sort of prank?' D. I. Hassan boomed.

'N-n-o!' Jack stammered. 'It must be here somewhere!' But he was starting to doubt himself. Had he sleepwalked back to the tree and stolen the money and spent it all on fast cars and fun without even knowing about it?

'Could anyone have seen you hiding the bag in here?' Emily asked.

Jack shook his head. But, hang on a minute, what if those graffiti guys had followed him, waited until he'd left and then stolen the bag? Jack gulped. He couldn't play for time any more. He was going to have to admit that he'd failed. The bag had gone. Slowly he backed out of the hollow tree and turned to face the expectant crowd. 'I, er, well, the thing is ...' he began.

But before Jack could go any further he heard a slobbery snuffling shuffling sound just behind him. The noise seemed familiar somehow. He turned round and came face to face with a goat ambling casually out from the other side of the hollow tree. But it wasn't just any goat! From the curly horns, the black and white markings and the long dopey face, Jack was sure it was his old friend from the night of the phantom lights. Its jaws worked from side to side as it chewed on something that hung from the sides of its mouth: something pink and beige and papery ...

'It's money!' Scott yelled, lunging at the goat. Emily, D. I. Hassan, the police officers and the photographer joined in and soon everyone was trying to tug the soggy fifty-pound notes from between the goat's big yellow teeth. Between them they extracted eleven notes, although several were heavily chewed and one was missing most of the queen's head.

Jack was just wondering whether the goat had already polished off the rest of the cash and the flask of diamonds and, if so, whether it was still technically his fault, when one of the uniformed officers called out from the bank of the nearby stream, where he'd been poking with a stick. 'Looks like the rest of it's over here,' he said, holding up the blue sports bag. Jack ran to his side and peered into the bag. *Yes!* The silver flask and two of the pizza boxes were still inside.

D. I. Hassan opened the flask and nodded. Then he opened the boxes. The money and diamonds were all intact.

The third pizza box was soon found lying open in the undergrowth, surrounded by a scatter of fifty-pound notes. After a short search all the cash was accounted for except for one note, which was presumably being digested in the goat's stomach.

D. I. Hassan stood up and brushed willow leaves from his trousers. 'Well, I suppose we can't arrest the goat for stealing fifty pounds!' he chuckled. 'We'll just have to put it down as his fee for finding the money for us!'

Jack put his arms around the goat's neck. 'Sorry we disturbed your lunch,' he said. 'I'm glad you weren't abducted by aliens, by the way,' he added in a low voice.

But not low enough. Scott had heard him. He thumped Jack's arm. 'You're not talking to that goat again, are you?' he laughed.

Jack thumped his brother back, but soon he and Emily were laughing too.

The goat bleated as if joining in the joke.

And, as for Drift, he ran round and round the tree. He'd found some squirrels to chase at last!

When Scott and Jack called at The Lighthouse the following morning they found Emily's parents in the guest lounge talking to Detective Inspector Hassan. Everyone was in a celebratory mood. It seemed that Emily's dad's reunion gig with his band was going ahead and tickets had already sold out, while the gallery in St Ives had decided to put on a massive show of her mum's paintings.

'I have a piece of good news, too,' D. I. Hassan said, smoothing the perfectly pressed trousers of his cream suit over his knees. 'Two pieces, in fact,' he added. 'We managed to trace that hotel key that you three found.'

'*I* found it on my own, actually,' Jack pointed out.

D. I. Hassan nodded and smiled at Emily. 'As you observed in your case notes, there are many hotels in Holland called The Yellow Tulip, but we've been able to identify this particular key as belonging to a small guesthouse in Amsterdam. Our Dutch police colleagues carried out a raid last night, and it turns out that The Yellow Tulip is the main headquarters for the Barrington gang's operations in Europe. They made a lot more arrests.'

'So the man who parachuted from the plane must have stayed at that guest house and dropped the key when he landed on the moor?' Jack asked.

'Precisely,' D. I. Hassan confirmed. 'In fact, we've also traced back connections between this gang and a well-known Dutch gun-smuggling crime ring that was operating thirty or forty years ago.'

Emily smiled. She couldn't wait to tell Miss Wendover. Perhaps it was the same gun-runners that the old lady had investigated when she was in Amsterdam in the 1970s. Miss Wendover had almost recovered from the flu now, and Emily was looking forward to telling her all about the successful outcome of Operation Phantom Lights.

'You said you had *two* pieces of news?' Scott asked D. I. Hassan.

D. I. Hassan smoothed down his moustache. He looked a little bashful all of a sudden. 'Ah, yes, I've been promoted. I'm Detective *Chief* Inspector now!'

Jack grinned. 'That must be because of all the crimes we've helped you solve on Castle Key.'

'Absolutely not!' D. C. I. Hassan said, but he looked very pleased as the friends congratulated him. 'Just remember,' he told them, 'it's important that you leave the police work to the professionals.'

'Of course,' Emily, Scott and Jack said with one voice. As far as they were concerned, they *were* professionals!

D. C. I. Hassan had only just left when Dotty arrived with an enormous box of Sven's prize-winning chocolate éclairs and more good news. 'Aidan is helping the police with information about the gang's activities,' she said, as Emily's mum handed her a cup of tea. 'He'll still be sent to prison for a short sentence, but he's promised to go straight after that. He's going to come and work for me at the café. Which reminds me, you're all entitled to free pizzas for life! It's the least I can do to thank you.' She reached across to stroke Drift, who was curled up on the sofa next to Emily. 'And free sausages for Drift, of course!'

Drift pricked up his ears. *Sausages?* After squirrels, *sausages* was his favourite word!

'Are you insane?' Scott asked. 'Have you any idea how many pizzas Jack can eat? You'll be bankrupt within weeks!'

Dotty laughed. 'Well, maybe I'd better just make it for a year then!'

—

The last visitor of the morning was Rosie Armitage.

The friends chatted with her for a long time about their exciting adventures together as they worked their way through the chocolate éclairs.

'Ooh, I almost forgot,' Rosie told Jack, handing him a book. 'I brought this for you. I know how much you love reading.'

Jack flicked through *The Moonrise Dragons*. Five hundred and fifty pages of miniscule writing and not a single picture! 'Cheers,' he said weakly.

'But that's not all,' Rosie said with a grin. 'Gran says she'll treat us all to a day out at Planet Adventure tomorrow.'

Jack was so excited he almost hugged her, but he didn't fancy being karate-chopped again so he punched the air instead. Planet Adventure was the most awesome theme park in Cornwall. He couldn't wait to go on the world-famous Obliterator ride! He jumped up and did a victory dance around the room. But as he passed one of the armchairs he noticed Emily's new school uniform hanging over the back. He stopped mid-shimmy.

There were only two more days of the summer holiday left.

Then he and Scott would be on the train back to London and school. It would be great to see Dad again, of course, but Jack hated having to leave Castle Key – and Emily and Drift – for a whole term.

Scott felt the same. 'We'll just have to make the most of our last two days,' he said bravely. 'What shall we do today?'

'How about body-boarding at West Rock Beach?' Jack said. 'Rosie, you can come too, of course!'

'Then we can borrow some ponies from Roshendra Farm and ride over the moor to Polhallow Lake,' Scott suggested.

'And paddle canoes to Willow Island,' Emily added.

'And then we could have a campfire at Chicken Bay,' Rosie joined in.

'We'll take some sausages and cook them for supper!' Jack said.

Sausages! Drift barked happily again.

Scott laughed. 'I think Drift's saying, *Can we stop off to chase some squirrels on the way?*'

'What are we waiting for?' Jack asked.

Emily grinned. 'You never know. We might just be able to squeeze another mystery into our last two days!'

Jack and Scott laughed. If anyone could, Emily could!

And after all, this *was* Castle Key.

There would always be another adventure waiting for them.

THE ADVENTURE CONTINUES

Secret agent tests
•
Character profiles
•
Hidden codes
•
Exclusive blogs
•
Cool downloads

DO YOU HAVE
WHAT IT TAKES?

Find out at
www.adventureislandbooks.com